THE MISSING HEIRESS MURDERS

Private eye Johnny Merak's latest client, top Mob man Enrico Manzelli, has received death-threats. A menacing man himself, he pressures Johnny to discover who was sending them — and why. Then Barbara Minton, a rich heiress, disappears, and her husband turns to Johnny. Despite Manzelli's ultimatum — that Johnny should focus on his case alone — he takes the job. But that's before he discovers the fate of the first detective Minton hired. And more bodies are stacking up . . .

JOHN GLASBY

THE MISSING HEIRESS MURDERS

Complete and Unabridged

LINFORD
Leicester

First published in Great Britain

First Linford Edition
published 2010

British Library CIP Data

Glasby, John S. (John Stephen)
    The missing heiress murders. - -
(Linford mystery library)
1. Merak, Johnny (Fictitious character)- -
Fiction. 2. Private investigators- -Fiction.
3. Gangsters- -Fiction. 4. Death threats- -
Fiction. 5. Heiresses- -Fiction. 6. Missing
persons- -Investigation- -Fiction.
7. Suspense fiction. 8. Large type books.
I. Title II. Series
823.9'14–dc22

ISBN 978–1–44480–457–7

Published by
F. A. Thorpe (Publishing)
Anstey, Leicestershire

Set by Words & Graphics Ltd.
Anstey, Leicestershire
Printed and bound in Great Britain by
T. J. International Ltd., Padstow, Cornwall

1

The Lady Disappears

I guess it all began when I walked into my office earlier than usual on that Monday morning. I'd spent the previous night with Jack Kolowinski, a sergeant in the LAPD. After a round of several bars in downtown L.A. it was almost three o' clock in the morning when I'd finally returned to my apartment. Waking after only a couple of hours' sleep, I decided to take a couple of painkillers and go into work — anything to take my mind off the pounding ache in my skull.

Business had been unusually quiet over the past couple of weeks. The temperature in the middle of the city was close to ninety degrees and all of the wrongdoers seemed to have migrated for the summer. No one was looking for errant husbands or wives and the Mobs were strangely quiet. It was almost as if everyone had got religion.

Leaning forward in my chair, I took the half-empty bottle of bourbon from the desk drawer and poured a slug into a glass. It was the wrong thing to do, of course. But at the time I couldn't think of anything better.

I was halfway through the drink when the sound of a car pulling up outside attracted my attention It wasn't usual for any clients to come calling so early in the day unless they had something extremely important on their minds or they preferred to drive around L.A. at a time when not too many people were around to notice them. Pushing back my chair I got up and went over to the window. What I saw I didn't like at all.

I recognized the type of automobile at once — a large black limousine like those used by the top men in the Organization. For one of these guys to come calling on me usually meant trouble, big trouble and I was the one who usually got it in the neck. Going back to my chair I sat down and waited for the knock on the door. It came a couple of minutes later.

'Come in,' I called. 'The door's open.'

The guy who stood there filled the entire doorway. He was the last person in the world I expected to see. Enrico Manzelli, Godfather of the entire L.A. Organization. As far as I was aware he never left his mansion several miles from the outskirts of town and, apart from his own handpicked men, no one ever saw Manzelli unless he sent for them. I realized I was staring at him in stunned surprise and closed my mouth at once. One had to be very careful where this man was concerned. One word he didn't like one wrong move, and you'd vanish as quickly as a snowflake in July.

Two more men came into the office. They were both tall, efficient looking guys. There would be guns concealed under their left arms and I knew they wouldn't hesitate to use them if Manzelli gave the word.

There was a chair in front of my desk and somehow Manzelli succeeded in lowering himself into it. His pants must have been oiled for him to accomplish the manoeuvre. The two henchmen stood on

3

either side of the door, saying nothing. They weren't here to talk.

'I trust you're not too busy to take on another client. Mister Merak,' Manzelli began smoothly. For a man of such large proportions his voice was singularly soft. Nevertheless, there was a touch of menace in it that sent a finger of ice brushing up and down my spine.

'Not at all. May I ask who this client might be and why he requires my help?'

He looked directly at me for a full minute without saying anything. I could feel his gaze boring into me. It wasn't a comfortable experience.

'I'm that client, Mister Merak. I must admit I never foresaw a time when I'd require the services of a private investigator for myself. But you've been useful to me in the past and I'm quite certain you know when to keep your mouth shut.'

'I'm glad to know you trust me,' I said.

His thick lips twisted into what might have been a smile. 'I don't. I trust no one. But I think you're well aware of what happens to anyone who might try to double cross me — or talk about any little conversation we may have.'

'I get the picture.' I leaned back, lit a cigarette, and tried to relax a little. It wasn't easy. I couldn't imagine what was coming next. The fact that Manzelli was actually sitting there in my office told me it had to be really big.

'Good. I suppose you've heard something of this new setup in the downtown quarter of the city?' His close-set eyes were really drilling into me now.

Stubbing out my cigarette, I said, 'You've lost me now. What setup is this?'

'You appear to know very little for a private detective. It's happening on your own doorstep and you know nothing about it.' Sarcasm dripped like honey from his voice. 'I presume you're acquainted with the name Cortega — Vinnie Cortega.'

The name sounded vaguely familiar but I couldn't place where I'd heard it before. I knew most of the Big Boys by name but Cortega wasn't one of them.

Manzelli sighed. I thought he leaned back in the chair but with his bulk I couldn't be sure. Placing the tips of his fingers together, he went on, 'I see I shall have to explain things to you, Merak. This man has just arrived in Los Angeles. My information is that he came across the border from Mexico about three months ago but originally he entered that country from Sicily. As far as I'm concerned he's already making a nuisance of himself.'

'In what way?' I asked.

At that moment I couldn't see how I could possibly be of any help to him. If anyone in the Organization stepped out of line, Manzelli only had to give the order and the offender suddenly dropped dead from lead poisoning or went for a dip in the ocean — all the way to the bottom.

'It would appear that he's set up some kind of protection racket without any consultation with the other families in the Organization. As you're doubtless aware, that is something I cannot allow to happen. It can so easily get out of hand and start big trouble.'

'But surely that isn't a job for a private investigator. You have your own boys to take care of things like that.'

He nodded ponderously. 'Of course,

you're quite right — I do. Unfortunately on this occasion there are — certain other problems.'

I took out another cigarette and lit it. I didn't like the way this conversation was going. 'Certain other problems?' I realized I was repeating myself.

'That is correct. I have recently received a number of death threats. It isn't the first time this has happened.' He waved a hand in a negligent gesture. 'A man in my position is bound to attract enemies. Normally, however, I would ignore such communications but these seem to have begun with the arrival of this man Cortega in L.A. You may say it's simply a coincidence but I do not believe in coincidences and therefore, knowing nothing about him whatsoever, I'm forced to take these threats very seriously.'

'I can understand that. I can also understand that you've no wish to bring the police into this.'

'Exactly. That is why I'm asking you to undertake this case for me. I want you to find out if Cortega is indeed behind these threats. Furthermore, I need to know everything about this racket he's operating. So far, no one seems willing to talk.'

'I'll certainly do my best,' I promised.

It didn't seem to bother him unduly that someone was planning to kill him. He appeared more concerned that things were taking place in the city about which he was completely in the dark.

'In addition,' he went on, 'none of what we've just discussed must go beyond these walls.'

'It won't,' I said. I was on the point of saying something more when the door opened and Dawn came in. I immediately noticed the expression of stunned shock on her face and guessed what she was thinking. These men were not the usual kind of visitors I got. Manzelli gave her the same kind of stare he'd given me while the two guys near the door moved their hands quickly towards their jackets.

'This is Dawn Grahame, my assistant,' I said hurriedly. 'She's helped me with a number of cases, some of which have been yours and I can assure you she'll say nothing of this meeting or you being here.'

Manzelli pondered that for a moment, obviously wondering whether to trust me or not. Then he got awkwardly to his feet, moving towards the door. Pausing there, he said softly to Dawn, 'Your employer clearly thinks very highly of you, Miss Grahame. I sincerely hope that trust isn't misplaced. Please heed my next words well. I've never been here. You've never seen me.'

Dawn nodded mechanically. Swallowing hard she stammered, 'I understand perfectly.'

'Just one more thing, Mister Merak.' He half turned to the man standing immediately behind him and snapped his fingers. The guy put his hand inside his jacket. For a moment I thought that, in spite of what he had just said, Manzelli meant to make sure we didn't talk. Then the guy brought out a newspaper, neatly folded.

'This is the early morning edition.' Manzelli went on smoothly. 'I think you'll find one of the items at the bottom of the center spread very interesting. It has only just happened so there are very few details at the moment. I'm well aware that you have a preference for cases with a touch of mystery to them. However, my advice on this particular occasion is not to get involved. There is the possibility it could be highly dangerous.'

Without elaborating on this enigmatic statement, he went out and the door closed softly behind them.

'Who was that?' Dawn asked. There was a quaver in her voice as if she had already guessed his identity.

I came back from the window, after watching the car drive away, and sat down. 'That was the Big Boss himself.'

'Manzelli?' Her voice was now no more than a scared whisper. 'Oh God — what did he want?'

'He's worried. I'd never have believed that Manzelli could be scared of anything. But he is now. Someone is out to kill him. There've been threats against his life before but he now reckons this is the real thing and he doesn't know who it is. The only lead he has is some new guy who's trying to muscle in on the Organization — a hood named Cortega. Apparently he's set up a protection racket somewhere in downtown L.A. It seems that Manzelli knows very little about it and that worries him. He usually knows everything that happens here and if anything goes on without his knowledge it could seriously undermine his authority.'

'So why has he come to see you?'

'He wants to know everything there is to know about Cortega and what he's planning. And it's up to me to find out for him.'

Dawn switched on the electric kettle. 'And how do you intend to go about it?' she asked. She still seemed stunned at meeting Manzelli face to face.

I lit a cigarette and waited until she brought the coffee over before speaking. 'First I want to know why he thinks it's important I should read what's in this paper.'

Opening it I immediately saw the headline. It was in small type and right at the bottom corner of the page. Quite clearly, as Manzelli had intimated, the news had only just come in before the paper had gone to press.

MULTI-MILLION DOLLAR
HEIRESS VANISHES

There was only a short paragraph. Evidently this news had only just broken and very few facts were known.

Dawn brought the coffee over and then stood at my shoulder staring down at the newspaper. All it said was that Barbara Minton, formerly Barbara Silworth, the wife of Edward Minton and heir to the multi-million dollar Silworth diamond empire had disappeared while driving home from a visit to her ill father in Colorado. Her car had been found ten miles from the nearest town on the Orange Freeway northeast of L.A. near the mountains. The vehicle had been totally burnt-out but there was no sign of any occupants.

I read the article twice; then shook my head. 'I don't see why Manzelli should warn me against getting involved in this mystery.' I said. 'Unless he has some prior knowledge that this Edward Minton is about to come here and ask me to look into it.'

Dawn pursed her lips and went back to her desk. Sipping her coffee, she said quietly, 'You're only assuming that Manzelli wants you to look into this case. Maybe he meant exactly what he said. Stay out of it and concentrate on finding out who it is has made these threats against him.'

'You could be right, Dawn, but somehow I don't think so.'

'All right then. Do you know anything about the Mintons, Johnny?'

'Not a thing. They aren't the kind of people who mix with folk like me.'

She smiled. 'But knowing you, Johnny, it's the kind of case you could get your teeth into rather than getting mixed up with these racketeers like Cortega.'

I finished my coffee. 'How would you fancy a drive out into the country?'

She looked surprised. 'Where are you thinking of going?'

'Maybe I'm just being plain stupid but I think I'll take a ride along the Orange Freeway.'

Her eyes widened. 'Whatever for? If you think about it this case has nothing to do with you — absolutely nothing. If Manzelli or the police find out you're investigating this incident just because you read it in the newspaper there could be hell to pay. You could even lose your license.'

'But don't you see, Dawn? There's something here that doesn't quite add up. Manzelli arrives, something he's never done before, and asks me to find out who it is wants him dead. When he puts it that way it's an order. You either do it or kiss the rest of your life goodbye.

'But then he brings this case to my notice. I've known Manzelli for some time. He's a very devious man. He only advises me to have nothing to do with this other case, warning me that it could be dangerous. That's his way of arousing my curiosity and making sure I look into it. After all, it's only just happened and I'd say that so far there's nothing for anyone to go on.'

'So notwithstanding all of this is mere speculation on your part you intend to get in first while any evidence is still there.'

'Something like that,' I admitted.

She digested that for a moment; then nodded. 'All right, Johnny. I'll go along with you but I still think you're wrong.'

Five minutes later I'd locked up the office and we were driving northeast towards the Orange Freeway. The traffic was pretty bad at first but as we proceeded, it lessened appreciably until, at times, we seemed to be the only ones on the road.

Dawn had been silent for quite a while but now she asked, 'Was there any mention in the paper of when the car was discovered?'

I shook my head. 'None at all. But it couldn't have been too long ago. Certainly there isn't much traffic on the Freeway but if it was a fire my guess is someone would notice it and inform the cops. It's pretty open country here.'

We drove on for another couple of miles and then I spotted the hold-up ahead of us. There was a thin plume of dark grey smoke hanging in the air like a blot on the landscape and I could just make out the tangled metal of the car. Several other vehicles were on the scene and a crowd of guys were gathered around the wreck. I noticed a couple of state troopers and the rest looked like the highway patrol.

I stopped as one of the cops stepped into the middle of the highway and held up his right hand. He came over and signalled to me to wind down the window.

'What's the trouble, officer?' I asked. He was a young guy and probably hadn't been too long in the force.

'We've had a vehicle fire, sir,' he said politely. 'I'm afraid the freeway is closed for the time being.'

'Was anyone hurt?' Dawn inquired innocently.

I thought the cop wasn't going to answer. But he did. 'No one killed or hurt, miss. In fact we found no one in the vicinity when we arrived.'

'Don't you think that's strange?' I asked.

'I guess so but there are a number of possibilities we're considering.'

'And you're sure the car's registered to Barbara Minton?'

16

'How did you know that, sir?'

'I read it in the early edition,' I told him. Taking out the newspaper from the glove compartment, I gave it to him.

Before the guy could say anything more one of the others, a tall, thin-faced man of around fifty, came over. I guessed he was someone pretty high up in the force and someone who wasn't going to take any nonsense.

'You seem to be unduly interested in this incident,' he said with more than a hint of suspicion in his tone. 'May I see some identification and your driver's license.'

I took them out of my wallet and handed them over. He perused them closely before giving them back. 'A private investigator, eh? So just why are you here, Mister Merak? Obviously you're not here simply out of morbid curiosity and you're quite a way out of town. You must have got wind of this fire from someone.'

Clearly, lying to this guy wasn't going to get me anywhere so I took a chance and said, 'I got the news from someone very high up in Los Angeles. Naturally I wouldn't dream of interfering in police business but my client seems to have the idea that somebody might need my help and ask me to take this case.'

The other's face took on a frosty expression. 'You say someone high up in L.A. Just how high up are we talking about?'

'I can't give his name, you understand. But I can say he lives in a very large mansion out in the country and, although he's very seldom seen outside, he has an interest in most everything that goes on in the city.'

His expression changed at once as I'd hoped it would. He sucked in a deep breath and gave a quick look around to make sure we couldn't be overheard. 'I get the picture,' he said in a low whisper, nodding. My wild card had paid off. He was acquainted, in some way, with Manzelli. He nodded again and held out his hand. 'I'm Lieutenant Morgan — homicide. I've heard of you, Merak, but I never expected you to be on this case so fast.'

'I'm not officially on the case, Lieutenant. In fact no one, apart from our mutual friend, has yet asked me to help in any way. It's only the fact that my client deliberately brought it to my attention that I'm here at all.'

I took back the newspaper from the young cop and stowed it away again. Then I got out of the car, motioning Dawn to do likewise. Now I was here I wanted to get as many details as possible. As I followed him towards the still smouldering wreckage, I wondered just what Manzelli's interest in this mystery was. I knew he'd have some kind of angle but I couldn't figure out what it was.

Beside me, Dawn wrinkled her nose as the smell of burning rubber hit us. Had anyone been inside this car once the fire started they'd have been fried to a crisp within minutes.

Those little mice inside my mind were now scampering around in crazy circles. They were telling me that the only possibilities that made any sense at all were that this fire had been started deliberately to destroy some kind of evidence and the driver was probably miles away by now — or Barbara Minton had been abducted and the kidnapper had torched the vehicle to destroy anything that might have been of value to the cops. They were also telling me that if Morgan was very well in with Manzelli I'd better be careful.

I gave the onlookers the once-over. There was a tall distinguished-looking guy standing on the other side of the tangled mess. Somehow, he looked lost and out of place. Morgan went over to him taking me with him, and touched his arm.

'This is Johnny Merak, a private investigator, Mister Minton,' he said. 'You may want to talk to him. Apparently he was told of this incident by a mutual friend of ours in L.A.'

Those little mice stopped their capering around at that remark. It could only mean that both these men were well in with Manzelli. I wondered if this was why Manzelli had warned me that having anything to do with the disappearance of Barbara Minton could be dangerous.

Minton eyed me up and down for a moment and then said, 'At the moment I already have a private investigator working for me, Mister Merak.'

'Doing what?' I asked.

For a moment I thought he didn't intend answering, thinking it was none of my business. Then he said thinly, 'If you must know I engaged him to check on my wife. I've had my suspicions about her for some time so I decided to discover whether any of the rumours I've heard are true or false.'

'And has he discovered anything?'

'Unfortunately, very little so far. However, he's only been working on the case for a couple of weeks so I've no intention of finishing him and taking on anyone else at the moment.'

'I understand. Since I'm here, however, may I take a look around? I gather this is your wife's car?'

He nodded. 'There's enough left of the registration plate for me to be absolutely certain. That's one of hers. She has another which is in the garage at home.'

'And she was driving back from visiting

her ill father in Colorado?'

'That is correct.'

'I see. Now that's what worries me. Why on earth was she taking this road? It would take her miles out of her way.'

No one said anything for a full minute. Then Morgan said harshly, 'Quite possibly she reckoned the traffic would be much lighter this way and she'd make better time. Maybe she liked this route with its view of the mountains. Who knows why she did it?'

'You could be right,' I nodded. 'It's just that I don't like any loose ends hanging. They're liable to trip you up.'

Neither man having raised any objections, I motioned to Dawn and said softly, 'You take a look around as well, Dawn. It's best to have two pairs of eyes. This is a woman's car and there may be something I'll miss.'

Bending, I examined the dashboard. The fire had been so fierce there wasn't much there that was recognisable. The speedometer, however, seemed fairly intact. The needle was stuck at ninety. That struck me as odd and I pointed it out to Lieutenant Morgan.

'Evidently at some point she must have been travelling at that speed,' he muttered off-handedly as if his thoughts were focussed on something else.

'But there are no skid marks on the road here,' I said, pointing. 'I'd say that tells us she braked normally at this point. If I were you I'd have someone check that instrument. It might provide some clues. Anyone doing ninety along this road would be taking their life in their hands.'

Leaning forward, I looked around the interior. Not that there was much to see. There was, however, something almost completely hidden beneath the passenger seat. Turning, to the Lieutenant, I pointed. 'Do you reckon one of your men can get that out? I've an idea what it is but I'd like to make sure. Be careful. This vehicle is still hot.'

Morgan motioned to one of the men standing close by.

It wasn't easy and it was ten minutes before the guy got the warped door open sufficiently to extricate it. As I'd suspected, it was a canister for holding petrol. Taking it well away from the wreck, the cop upended it. It was empty.

'So either she brought a spare can of gas with her in case she ran out and couldn't get to a gas station.' I observed, 'or it was brought with the deliberate intention of setting fire to this vehicle.'

'If you want my opinion,' Morgan said, 'I'd say the latter is the more likely.'

'I agree with you,' I nodded. Moving away from the wreck, I examined the surrounding area. All of that in the vicinity of the wreck was scorched and blistered and yielded no clues. Some distance away, however, I noticed two sets of footprints in the damp ground and pointed them out to the lieutenant.

'We'd noticed those,' he said. 'Evidently a man and a woman wearing high heels.'

'Then the question that occurs to me is — was she going with him willingly — or not? If she went willingly then I'll bet my bottom dollar she was in with whatever plan they'd concocted between them.'

Minton didn't look too happy at that remark. 'I can assure you, Mister Merak, my wife was alone when she left her parents' house. I checked that before I left with the police to come here.'

'Then we have a problem,' I told him. 'Either she picked up someone on the way between here and Colorado — or this stranger was waiting here for her. That doesn't seem likely to me.'

'Why not?' Morgan asked.

I waved an arm to encompass the scenery around us. 'Look around you. There's nothing here for miles. Wherever he came from he'd have to walk because there's no sign of any other vehicle nearby.'

Morgan rubbed his chin. 'There's one other possibility. Someone could have dropped him off at this spot and then driven on.'

I had to admit he had a point there. But I didn't like the idea of introducing more people than absolutely necessary into the scenario. At the moment we were all stumbling around in the dark with few real facts to go on.

Going back to the wreck I walked slowly around it twice, taking in every detail. I had the feeling we were missing something but I couldn't figure out what it was. Finally, I turned to Dawn who stood watching me. 'I guess there's nothing more to see here. We'd better be getting back into town.'

Minton came forward as I walked towards my own car. 'If you've no objection, Mister Merak, I'd like your card just in case I want to get in touch with you. Something has happened here which I'm at a loss to understand. I may need your services in the future.'

I took my card from my wallet and gave it to him. He perused it for a few moments and then slipped it into his jacket pocket. I walked back to my car. Slipping behind the wheel I waited until Dawn got in, then edged the Merc away from the scene. Manzelli had figured it right when he'd implied I'd be interested in this case. But there were still many loose ends dangling and no common denominator to link any of them together. I had the impression that everyone was holding something back from me and I didn't like that.

In the office, Dawn put the electric

kettle on. 'I guess you could do with a strong coffee.'

'I could,' I acknowledged. 'As strong as you care to make it. This case has got me stymied at the moment but there has to be some logic behind what we saw.'

I'd almost finished my drink when the phone rang. Swinging my legs off the desk I picked up the receiver. It was Lieutenant O'Leary. He didn't sound his usual happy self but maybe that was because it was Monday morning or he'd got out of bed the wrong side.

'I've just had a colleague of mine on the phone — a Lieutenant Morgan,' he said sharply. 'It seems you've been out to the Orange Freeway checking on an accident there.'

'I happened to be driving along that route,' I said.

'Don't try to be funny with me, Merak.' His tone was definitely antagonistic now. 'Where you're concerned, you don't just happen to be anywhere. Who put you on to this? It's only just been mentioned in the early edition.'

I thought fast. Any mention of Manzelli

and I could be in big trouble. I decided to dodge around his question 'Just what is this incident to you, Lieutenant? It happened outside your area of jurisdiction. This is Lieutenant Morgan's case.'

'Perhaps. But since both you and the Mintons live in the city, I also happen to have an interest in it. And where you are concerned I'm the one asking the questions.'

'O.K. Lieutenant, I understand. So why are you ringing me?'

'That's better. Now, have you been asked by anyone to look into Barbara Minton's disappearance?'

'No.'

'That's what I figured. But I think it's likely you will be in the very near future.'

'Why do you say that?' I had the feeling O'Leary knew something I didn't. His next words confirmed this.

'Do you know a guy called James Baker?'

'Baker? No, I've never heard of him.'

'It seems he's in your line of business — or was until last night.'

'A private investigator?'

'That's right. He'd just been hired by Minton to keep an eye on his wife.'

'So why are you telling me all this?'

There was a pause. Then O'Leary said, 'He was found dead in his office late last night, shot through the head with a heavy calibre weapon.'

That really hit me. This case had seemed odd in the beginning but now it was getting sinister.

'You got any suspects, Lieutenant?'

'None at the moment. That's why I want you here right now. You seem to have pushed yourself into this case whether anyone wants you or not.'

I took a pen from my pocket and pulled the newspaper towards me. 'Just give me the address and I'll be there in fifteen minutes,' I said. After he'd given it, I put the phone down and looked across at Dawn.

'That was O'Leary,' I told her. 'It seems that the private detective Minton hired to follow his wife won't be doing the job any more. He's dead.'

Dawn raised her delicately-shaped eyebrows in mute inquiry.

'He's been discovered in his office, shot with a heavy calibre weapon. O'Leary wants me there — pronto.'

'Finish your coffee and I'll come with you, Johnny. Like you said earlier, two pairs of eyes are better than one.'

I didn't argue with her. When she made up her mind to do something I doubted if the President could dissuade her.

The address O'Leary had given me was in the lower-class areas of L.A. The paint was peeling from the walls and the stairs creaked ominously under our feet as we went up to the third floor. The sign on the door said: JAMES BAKER PRIVATE INVESTIGATOR.

I pushed the door open and went inside with Dawn following closely on my heels. The office was a mess. Papers were strewn across the floor and it was clear someone had given the place a good going-over. There'd obviously been something of importance here that someone wanted badly. O'Leary and Sergeant Kolowinski were both there together with a little guy in shirtsleeves. I guessed he was the owner of the place. There was a desk near the window and a body lying slumped across it. Blood had puddled across the scratched surface.

O'Leary looked up at me as I went in and approached the desk. He jerked a thumb towards the little guy. 'This is the landlord of this place,' he said shortly. 'It seems the phone went for Baker about fifteen minutes after this guy got in. When it kept ringing he came to see if there was anything wrong and found the place like this.' He turned to the little guy. 'All right, you can go now.'

After the guy had gone, I looked down at the body. Both hands were on the desktop and there was a large automatic clutched tightly in his right hand.

'How do you figure this, Lieutenant?' I asked. 'Suicide?'

'It certainly looks that way to me. Maybe he had money worries or this case he'd taken on for Minton was getting the better of him. Why — what's your opinion?'

'From what I can see I've no doubt he was murdered.'

'Now why the hell do you say that?' I

could see I'd just upset his nice cosy little suicide theory. 'I'll bet we only find his prints on that gun with just one slug fired into the right side of the head.'

'Sure you will. But there's one thing you haven't noticed.'

'Oh, what's that?'

Easing the body back into the chair I flipped open his jacket. 'The holster for that gun is under his right arm. He was left-handed and it's virtually impossible to shoot yourself in the right side of the head holding the weapon in your left hand.'

O'Leary uttered a long sigh. 'O.K. You've convinced me.' He glanced at Kolowinski. 'We have a murder on our hands, Sergeant.'

'One thing is quite obvious, Lieutenant,' I interrupted. 'Whoever did this must have rendered him unconscious first. He wouldn't just sit there and allow someone to take his gun and shoot him in the head. I'd say it was someone he knew who slipped him something in that coffee.'

I pointed to the empty cup near the

edge of the desk. 'It will have been washed by now so I doubt if you'll find any traces left.'

'I'll do that,' O'Leary said. He glanced towards the safe in the wall. Going over to it he checked it then went on, 'I'll get someone to open it. There may be something important inside.'

'Don't you need a search warrant for that, Lieutenant?' Dawn queried.

O'Leary gave her a look that seemed to sizzle through the air. 'In case you haven't been listening, Miss Grahme, this is now a murder scene. Furthermore your guy is dead and in no position to make any complaint.'

Dawn gave a nod and said nothing more.

O'Leary pushed his hat back further on his head. 'The way I figure it somebody didn't want this guy to go on with his investigations. Either someone had a grudge against him or he was getting a little too close to the truth.'

'That would seem to make Barbara Minton the main suspect,' Dawn spoke up again.

The Lieutenant gave her a sharp glance. 'Why do you say that, Miss Grahame?'

'She was the one he was investigating. If he discovered she was having an affair that wouldn't sit very well with her husband, would it?'

'No, perhaps not,' O'Leary agreed reluctantly. 'At the moment, however, we'll be looking at every line of inquiry. In the meantime, is there anything more you want to see here?' He looked directly at me.

I shook my head. 'Not right now. But I would like to know what the contents of that safe are once you get it open.'

O'Leary considered that. I knew he wasn't sure how deeply I was involved in this case. To be quite truthful, I wasn't even sure myself. 'Very well,' he said finally. 'And as for what happened out of town I want you to keep me informed. Something in here — ' He tapped the side of his head meaningfully, ' — tells me that both of these incidents are connected in some way.'

'I couldn't agree more, Lieutenant,' I

said as I moved away from the desk. Opening the door I went down the stairs with Dawn at my heels. Things were now happening too fast for my liking. If Minton did ask me to take the case there were a lot of things I'd like to have asked Baker. Now, with him dead, not only wouldn't I get any answers, but a lot more questions had suddenly popped up.

Dawn sat in silence as we drove back to the office. I knew she was just as puzzled as I was. There was nothing about what had happened that was simple and straightforward. First there was Manzelli. Just where did he come into it? Then Barbara Minton vanishing with some stranger on her way home leaving her car a burnt-out wreck on a road she would not normally have taken. And now the detective her husband had hired to check on her was slumped over his desk with a bullet in his brain.

Somewhere there had to be a logical explanation for all of this but I was damned if I could see it. It wasn't until we were both sitting down that Dawn voiced my own thoughts. 'This whole affair doesn't make any sense, Johnny.'

'Manzelli knows something that he's not telling me. But there's no way I can ask him.'

'If you want my advice, which you probably don't, I'd forget this case and concentrate on what Manzelli asked you to do. I — '

There was no chance for her to say anything more for at that moment the phone rang. Twisting in my chair I picked up the receiver. 'Merak,' I said.

A voice I didn't recognize said, 'You don't know me, Mister Merak, but it's imperative I should speak to you.'

'O.K. Do you know where my office is?'

There was a pause and then the caller went on, 'Not your office. That's where they'd expect me to go.'

That started warning bells ringing in my mind. Anyone who was scared to come to the office for fear of being followed was usually running away from something and that usually meant the cops or the Mob.

'Who would expect you to come here?'

I asked, not really expecting a truthful answer.

'I can't tell you that over the phone. All I can say is that it concerns someone who's recently disappeared.'

I made up my mind right away. 'All right then. Where do you suggest we meet?'

'Do you know the park on the north side of town?'

'I know it.'

'I'll meet you there in half an hour.'

'All right. How will I know you?'

There was another short pause, then he said, 'Don't worry about that, Mister Merak. I know you.'

The line went dead and I sat staring at the receiver in my hand for a full minute before putting it down.

Dawn looked across at me. 'Who was that? Not Manzelli again?'

'No. Some guy who reckons he knows something about Barbara Minton's disappearance. He won't come here but wants me to meet him in the park on the north side.'

'You want me to come with you? It could be a trap.'

'You worry about me too much,' I told her, shaking my head at her proposal. 'Besides, whoever he is, he won't do anything in the middle of the park. There are too many folk around. Besides, I have this.' I patted the holster beneath my jacket.

I'd just reached the door when the phone rang again. It was a woman's voice and again it was one I'd never heard before. 'Is that Mister Merak, the private investigator?'

'It is,' I replied.

'This is Ophelia Silworth. I understand you're investigating my daughter's disappearance. I believe that a certain James Baker who was investigating her on behalf of her husband, Edward Minton, has just been murdered. May I ask if there's any truth in this?'

I hesitated. It seemed a funny question for her to ask and I wasn't sure how to answer her. Finally, I said, 'I'm afraid this is something I can't talk about at the moment. I suggest you get in touch with Lieutenant O'Leary of the L.A.P.D. He can tell you a lot more than I can.'

I put the phone down.

2

Strange Disclosures

I got to the park twenty minutes later and parked the car just inside the gates. The place seemed more crowded than usual for a weekday. Several kids were kicking a ball about as I walked towards the spot where a fountain formed a rainbow of prismatic colours.

As I walked I closely studied the faces of the people who passed me on either side. This guy I was supposed to meet had said that I didn't know him. But the way I figured it was if he knew me sufficiently well to recognize me in a crowd it was possible he might be somebody from my past.

There were half a dozen wooden benches placed in a neat circle around the pond. A couple were already occupied so I chose the one furthest from them. I reckoned the guy I was to meet might want to give any information he had in strict confidence and wouldn't want anyone else listening in. I'd been there for only a few minutes when my supposed informant arrived. I spotted him when he was twenty feet away and recognized him at once. It was Edward Minton!

I had the feeling there was something odd about him being there. I never forget a voice and that voice I'd heard on the phone had not belonged to the guy I'd met that morning on the Orange Freeway.

He sat down beside me and said in a low voice, 'I must apologize for the little game on the phone, Mister Merak. That was one of my servants who spoke to you.'

'May I ask the reason for the subterfuge?'

'Certainly. I think you've already guessed that James Baker was working for me. They said at first that it was suicide, that he'd shot himself in the head with his own gun. Now, however, they believe it was murder. If that's true I wasn't sure you'd be willing to accept this case and take over where he left off. I wanted to be sure you'd come here and let me talk to you.'

'And have you spoken about Baker to anyone else?'

'Certainly not. I've told no one.'

I turned the idea of accepting the case over in my mind. The fact that Baker had been killed, possibly because he was getting a little close to the truth, didn't particularly bother me. I'd taken on jobs for the Mobs in the past and things don't get more dangerous than that.

'I take it that you hired him because you had certain suspicions about your wife. You reckon she's cheating on you. Did he ever get any proof from Baker that she was having an affair?'

He pursed his lips into a thin line of concentration before saying, 'Nothing that would stand up in a divorce court, I'm afraid.'

'I see. And what makes you think I'd be any more successful than he was?'

'I'm quite a good judge of character, Mister Merak, although in Baker's case he was recommended to me by a friend.

But even though it's only been a short time since we met this morning, it's been long enough for me to have made a few inquiries about you. What I've learned, I like. I know you spent many years inside the Organization as a petty crook; that you even spent three years in San Quentin.'

'I was framed for that,' I said.

Whether he believed me or not I couldn't tell. However, it didn't seem to bother him. 'Then may I take it that you'll accept this case for a ten thousand dollar retainer and twice your usual expenses.'

He took an envelope from his jacket pocket and handed it to me. 'I also want to know exactly what happened this morning. I've never been unfaithful to Barbara. I've given her everything she wanted. There's also a recent photograph of her.'

'Thanks. That may help a lot.' I stuffed the envelope into my jacket pocket.

'All right, if she's grown tired of me and wants a divorce, I can understand that. But why disappear like this and in this odd fashion? There must be a reason for her acting like this but I'm damned if I can figure it out. Maybe you can.'

'At the moment I must admit I'm as puzzled as you are. There are so many questions needing to be answered that I'm not sure where to begin. Some of these questions relate to you so it's important you tell me the truth, otherwise I can't help you.'

He sat quite still for a long moment, staring at the ground beneath his feet. Then, looking straight at me, he said: 'I've nothing to hide. Ask your questions and I'll do my best to answer them.'

'From what I hear, your wife is a very wealthy woman in her own right. It may be that she's dead and her body is hidden someplace. Where the cops are concerned, that would make you the prime suspect since I presume you'd inherit everything.'

If he felt shocked by what I'd said, he gave no outward sign of it. Instead, he said evenly, 'I'm afraid you're quite wrong on that point. My wife insisted I sign a pre-nuptial agreement before we married.

If she were to die, all I'd get would be the house and a small quantity of jewels that I've always admired.'

'And the rest of her dough?'

'That goes to some charity she formed some years ago. I don't know anything about that, I'm afraid. So you see, it's not in my interests to murder her as you're suggesting.'

'Then I guess that would put you a little lower down my list of suspects. However, since we've no proof that she's dead, we'll let that pass for the moment. Have you ever cheated on her?' I shot the question at him, watching for any reaction. There was none beyond an emphatic shake of his head.

I believed him. He didn't look the kind of man who'd play around. He seemed like one of those religious guys who believed that marriage vows were for life.

'Anything else?' he asked.

'Just one thing. Can you give me any specific reasons why you should believe she's cheating on you?'

He thought that over for a while before

replying. Leaning forward, his elbows resting on his knees, hands clasped tightly together, he said, 'Some time ago, she took to going out late at night. When I questioned her about it she claimed that an old friend from back East had just arrived in L.A. and she went to visit her at times. I asked her the name of this friend and where she was staying but she wouldn't tell me.'

'So the suspicions started in your mind that she was seeing some other guy?'

'Not at first. I wanted to trust her. But — ' He hesitated.

'Go on,' I prompted.

'One night I decided to follow her. She drove to this restaurant on the other side of town. There was this man seated at one of the tables on the far side of the room. She went in and sat with him and it was obvious they were more than mere friends.'

'I get the picture. All right, I'll take the case. If I do find anything, I'll get in touch with you right away.'

He got up. 'I'm sure you'll do your best. I look forward to hearing from you when you've anything to report. Anyone will tell you where I live.'

I watched him walk away. Feeling the envelope into my inside pocket, I thought: There goes a man who has a lot more to hide than he's willing to tell. Perhaps it would be wise to probe into his affairs before I started on his wife.

Accordingly, once I got back to the office I asked Dawn to find out everything she could on Edward Minton. While she was gone I sat with my legs up on the desk trying to figure out which of these cases I should get my teeth into first. Commonsense and self-preservation told me I should deal with Manzelli. But it was early days and so many things had happened. I told myself it would be better to take one thing at a time and stick with the missing Barbara Minton.

Dawn arrived back half an hour later. Judging by the pile of notes she had I guessed she'd found out quite a lot about Edward Minton and suggested we go for an early lunch when she could fill me in on the details. We found a little Italian restaurant just a couple of blocks from

46

the office. There were few customers at that hour and we'd no difficulty finding a table near the door.

While we ate Dawn gave me the lowdown on everything she'd discovered concerning Edward Minton. Apparently, he'd set up a chain of hardware stores throughout the city and was a reasonably wealthy man when he met and married Barbara Silworth. They'd been together for more than fourteen years and accordingly to all reports the marriage was reasonably happy. There was no doubt, however, that Barbara Minton was the partner who had the real dough.

Dabbing her lips with the napkin, Dawn went on, 'There were rumours about an affair that happened some nine years ago.'

'On whose part?' I asked.

'His. His wife had been suspicious for some time and when she finally found some letters from this other woman she confronted him with them.'

'Did he try to deny it?'

'Apparently not. He must have realized the game was up and admitted it.

Naturally he swore it wouldn't happen again. I'm not sure whether or not she believed him or really forgave him but they continued to live together.'

Leaning back I took out my cigarettes and offered one to Dawn and lit it for her. 'So Barbara stayed on and to all appearances remained the loving wife. But why did he lie to me about that? He claimed he'd never cheated on her and I must say he sounded convincing.'

'Maybe it was nothing more than malicious gossip,' Dawn suggested.

I'd come across similar situations before. With all her dough and knowing what she did there was no doubt she was controlling him, watching his every move. Sometimes that could end in murder.

'There's something else which may interest you, Johnny. Minton has been well in with Sam Rizzio for several years.'

I nodded. 'That doesn't surprise me. He certainly knows Enrico Manzelli well enough. He as good as admitted it this morning. I wonder what his racket is with Rizzio?'

Dawn closed her notebook. 'Somehow

I don't think either Minton or Rizzio will tell you that.'

The coffee came and I sipped it slowly trying to put my chaotic thoughts into some kind of order. It wasn't easy. Even now, with what little information I had, I knew it would be far from straight forward. I now had two cases to work on and although I'd no real evidence to go on, I had the funny feeling they were connected in some way.

I put the idea to Dawn but after a few moments reflection she said, 'I can't see any way in which these two cases can be connected, Johnny. My guess is that Edward Minton is right and his wife has gone off with this man she's been seeing for some time. But there's no way you can bring this mobster Cortega into it.'

I let it go at that. Those little mice were telling me I should spend some time concentrating on one case at a time. I didn't want to get mixed up with someone like Cortega at the moment so I decided on the missing Barbara Minton. Even with that case, however, there seemed to be plenty of clues just lying around but several of them didn't make any sense. What had happened at that lonely spot on the Orange Freeway? I wondered.

The evidence said that Barbara had driven alone to that place where some guy had turned up — exactly how I didn't know — and after torching the car they'd both walked off into the open country. That was where the funny part came in. Why hadn't this stranger arrived in a car, picked her up after the deed had been done, and driven off with her? And then there was Baker's murder that had been made to look like suicide. Who had killed him — and why? I doubted if it had been Minton. He had no reason to kill the guy he'd hired to check on his wife.

I paid the check and we left, walking back to the office where I found someone waiting for me. It was Lieutenant Morgan. Unlocking the door. I let him in. Sitting down, I asked, 'Have you got anything more on Barbara Minton, Lieutenant?'

Taking off his hat, he placed it on the

desk. 'Nothing at all, I'm afraid. I've put out an APB on her but so far they've turned up nothing.'

'But there is something more,' I said, 'Otherwise you wouldn't be here.'

'A couple of things I think you may find interesting.' He fished inside his jacket pocket and brought something out, tossing it across the desk to me. It was an envelope and there were a couple of photographs inside, both of Barbara's burnt-out car but taken from different angles. 'The other thing is that there was another car at the scene.'

I looked up sharply at that. 'But we saw nothing there to indicate that — '

'It seems we didn't look far enough at the time,' he interrupted. 'One of my men made his way along the freeway for half a mile. There was evidence that a car had come from the direction of town, stopped, and then made a U-turn.'

So that explained one point that'd been worrying me. It seemed clear what had happened. Barbara's accomplice had parked well away from the fire so as to throw us off the track and make us believe the two of them had walked into the open country together.

'But we still have no idea where she is now and who this stranger is,' I said.

Morgan gave a brief nod of agreement. 'We'll keep looking,' he asserted thinly. 'L.A. is a big place but unless they're in with the Organization, we'll find them. Do you reckon those photographs will tell us anything?'

'I can't think of anything we overlooked at the scene,' I said, examining them closely. Dawn came over and put a hand on my shoulder, staring down intently at the pictures. 'I guess these pictures were taken before Dawn and I arrived on the scene. The empty gas can is still visible beneath the passenger seat and — '

'That's correct,' Morgan interrupted.

Looking closely at the photographs I had the sudden feeling that something about them didn't add up. For a moment I couldn't figure out what it was. Then it hit me.

'That's very peculiar,' I said, half to myself. 'I've only just realized it.'

Morgan looked puzzled. 'Realized what?'

'That gas canister. It was empty when we got it out.'

'That's right,' he agreed. 'What of it?'

'We all figured she'd brought a full can of gas with her and it was used to start the fire. But if that's the case, why douse the car with gas and then put the empty can under the seat before starting the fire? Surely the sensible thing to do would be to simply toss it away. It doesn't make sense.'

Morgan rubbed his chin and stared at me across the desk. 'You're right. I never thought of that. Unless she hoped it would be destroyed in the blaze along with the rest of the evidence.'

Leaning back, I said, 'I don't buy that, Lieutenant. To make sure of that all she have to do was throw it onto the seat, not place it carefully under it.'

'Then you've got me beat. I can't think of any logical reason why she'd do that. Could be she did it without thinking.'

'Suppose — ' Dawn began. She hesitated.

'Go on.' Morgan urged. 'I'm willing to listen to anything at the moment, no matter how fantastic it might seem.'

'Well, suppose there never was any gas in that canister. Perhaps it contained something else; something Barbara Minton considered important or valuable.'

Morgan considered that, finally saying, 'Well if you're right it must have been something quite small that she obviously took with her.'

'Diamonds?' I suggested.

The Lieutenant drummed with his fingers on the desk. 'Now that's a possibility,' he agreed. 'Her father runs this diamond empire and she could quite easily have taken some, possibly to give to this man she met either as a present or a blackmail payment.'

I had to agree it all made a crazy kind of sense. But it was all mere speculation.

After Morgan had left I decided to pay another visit to Baker's office. It would be taped off as a crime scene but I reckoned I might be able to talk my way inside, even if O'Leary was still present. I left Dawn to continue her checking on Vinnie Cortega. I didn't want Manzelli thinking I was ignoring him. That would be bad for business and my health.

As I expected there was a cop standing outside the door of Baker's office. I showed him my business card, saying, 'I'm now working for Edward Minton as a private investigator. The guy who was murdered here had that job until he was rubbed out and I need to get hold of any records relating to Minton's case.'

'I'm afraid nothing can be removed from here without Lieutenant O'Leary's permission, sir.' The cop was polite but he wasn't about to let me get my hands on Baker's notes.

'Where's the Lieutenant?' I asked.

'He went back to the precinct about an hour ago. He should be back any minute if you'd care to wait.'

There was nothing else I could do but wait. Two cigarettes later O'Leary arrived. He gave me a frosty look and snapped, 'You again. What the hell do you want, Merak?'

'Edward Minton has hired me to take over from the late Mister Baker.'

'So?'

'So if possible I'd like to get hold of any

notes Baker may have made concerning Barbara Minton. It would also help me if you told me what you found in that safe.' I indicated the safe, the door of which was now open.

'All of the dead man's papers are down at the precinct,' O'Leary said thinly. 'As for the contents of that safe, all we found was several hundred dollars in small bills.'

'And when do you reckon I can get his case notes?'

O'Leary shrugged. 'I've got a couple of men going through them at the moment. There might be a clue there to the identity of his killer. You can have them once my men are finished.'

'Thanks.' It was probably the best I could hope for. 'Do you mind if I take a look around this place?'

I expected him to say no, merely adding that this was police business and he didn't want me poking my nose into it. Instead, he gave a nod. 'Help yourself. But I don't think you'll find anything important. We've been over everything twice.'

'Has everything been dusted for prints?' I asked.

'Like I said, we've been over the lot.'

I checked that the safe was empty and then went through the drawers in Baker's desk. There wasn't much, just a few papers. I skimmed through them quickly. None of them made any reference to Minton. Evidently O'Leary hadn't bothered with them. I was on the point of putting them back when I noticed a name scrawled on one of them. It was a name I recognized immediately. Benny Lesser.

When Sean Malloy, head of the Malloy outfit had been murdered some weeks earlier by Edith Somerville, Benny had taken over the gang. I doubted if O'Leary was aware of this and that was the reason why this piece of paper meant nothing to him. To me, however, it could mean a lot. If Baker had somehow been mixed up with the Malloys it might explain why he had been shot. I stuffed the sheet of paper into my jacket pocket while O'Leary had his back turned to me.

Breaking off his conversation, the Lieutenant turned to face me. 'Have you seen enough, Merak?' His tone implied that he didn't want me there any longer than was necessary.

'I'm finished,' I told him.

'Did you find anything?' he asked as I walked to the door.

'Nothing important. I'll drop into the precinct later for those notes if your men have finished with them.'

*   *   *

Five o'clock and I locked up the office and went down the stairs to the Merc sitting at the kerb. Dawn had insisted on preparing a meal for us that evening and had gone back to her place on the strict understanding that I arrived there within half an hour after I'd picked up Baker's notes.

Sergeant Kolowinski was sitting behind the front desk when I arrived. He got up and gave me a friendly nod. 'The Lieutenant told me you'd be coming in for some papers we took from Baker's office,' he said. 'I'll get them for you. The boys have finished with them.'

He went through into the back, returning five minutes later with a large bundle of files that he placed on the desk in front of me. 'Seems there's not much in them,' he commented, pushing them towards me. 'I don't know what you hope to find there Johnny.'

'Maybe nothing,' I told him. 'It's just a hunch I've got. He knew something important. That's why he was murdered. It's now up to me to find out what it was.'

He grinned. 'Then I wish you luck, Johnny.'

'Thanks, Jack,' I said. I knew what he meant. Judging by the number of files it would take me a week to go through them all.

Dawn was in the kitchen when I let myself into her apartment. There was the smell of roast chicken in the air and it reminded me I'd eaten nothing since morning. I passed her some of the files and while we ate we both searched through them for any reference to Barbara Minton. Fortunately, Baker had been a very meticulous man, jotting down details of his various cases in a neat style of handwriting that was easy to follow.

Finally, we laid the files on one side and compared notes. Despite the fact that Baker had only been on the Minton case for a couple of weeks or so, he'd found out quite a lot. Barbara Minton was undoubtedly meeting someone behind her husband's back. Nowhere, however, was there any mention of this man's name, no clue as to his identity.

Seemingly the two of them would meet in the Golden Flamingo casino near the front where this guy was apparently something of a gambler, often losing several thousand dollars during a night's play. My guess on reading this was that most, if not all of this dough, was Barbara's. She, however, rarely played the tables, preferring just to stand and watch.

Their other regular meeting place was the Kelton Hotel where they often stayed the night together. Judging from what we'd just read it seemed that Baker had been on the ball where this case was concerned. And the evidence was leading me to suspect either Barbara or her mysterious companion of his murder.

Dawn lit a cigarette and said pointedly, 'Our problem with these notes is that there aren't any photographs of the two together.'

'Unless Baker was being very careful and kept anything like that separate from his notes,' I suggested. 'It's what I'd have done.'

'Then where are they? Do you reckon O'Leary took them?'

I shook my head emphatically. 'I don't believe the Lieutenant has them. It's more likely the murderer found them and took them.'

'A pity,' Dawn murmured. 'Then we might know what he looks like.'

'There might still be a way of doing that.'

'How, Johnny? You've got something in mind?'

'Yeah. I think we should pay a visit to the Golden Flamingo casino. It's just possible someone there might remember them.'

★   ★   ★

61

It was quite late in the evening when Dawn and I entered the Golden Flamingo. It was another of the large casinos run by the Organization and from what I'd heard Sam Rizzio had a pretty big stake in it. As one of the topmost operators in L.A. he had a finger in most everything.

Already, the place was crowded with folk who believed this was their lucky night when they'd hit the jackpot. It was far more likely they'd leave without enough to pay for a cab back home. We'd only been in the place for a couple of minutes when I noticed Rizzio standing close to one of the roulette tables. I didn't have time to warn Dawn. He'd already spotted me and was walking over.

His lips parted in what was supposed to be a smile of welcome but I'd seen more friendly grins on the tigers at the zoo. I'd saved him from the chair once when his boss, Carlos Galecci, had been murdered but like most of his kind he had a very short memory. In particular, he didn't like people like me on the premises just in case I uncovered something he'd prefer hidden.

'Johnny Merak,' he said, shaking my hand. 'I haven't seen you around for a long time. How are things in the private investigation business?'

'Pretty good,' I told him. 'I suppose you've heard that Barbara Minton has mysteriously disappeared.'

'I've heard rumours,' he said thinly. 'Are you on that case?'

I nodded. 'I've heard that she sometimes comes here with some guy who isn't her husband. Seems this guy is something of a gambler but she just stands and watches.'

His eyes narrowed at that. 'I reckon you listen to too many rumours, Johnny. As far as I'm aware she's never been in this place. You sure you haven't got the Golden Flamingo mixed up with some other gambling joint?'

I looked him straight in the eyes. 'Now why should the fact that Barbara Minton would come in here worry you so much, Sam? From what I've heard of her she'd bring a touch of class to this place.'

Rizzio remained silent for a full minute and I knew he was trying to reach a

63

decision about something. Then he seemed to have made up his mind for he jerked a thumb towards the door behind him and said, 'Come with me. I may be able to help you. You can bring your lady friend unless she'd care to try her luck at one of the tables.'

Dawn shook her head and followed me as Rizzio led the way into a small office. He motioned us to a couple of chairs.

'You've done me a couple of good turns in the past, Johnny, so I'll be straight with you. I met this dame about two years ago. You say she doesn't gamble now. O.K. I'll take your word for it but believe me she did when I knew her. She came in here and a couple of other casinos every single night. Roulette, faro, dice, you name it she was up for it. She'd lose twenty thousand in a single night and think nothing of it.'

Rizzio leaned back and took out a golden cigarette case. He offered one to Dawn and myself. Lighting mine I blew smoke into the air

'So why did she suddenly stop?' I asked.

'One night she really went to town. By the end of the night she must have lost fifty thousand dollars. She didn't have that kind of dough on her and asked me to take an IOU. Naturally, I figured her good for the money so I accepted it.'

'Are you saying she welshed on the deal?' Dawn spoke up for the first time.

Rizzio nodded. 'When I asked her for the dough she laughed in my face, told me to take her to court. She said that with her connections they'd believe her rather than a mobster.'

He leaned forward and rested his elbows on the desk. 'You know me well enough, Johnny, to know that nobody takes me for a fool and insults me to my face.'

'So what did you do?'

'I sent the IOU to her father. He paid up in full and my guess is he threatened to cut her out of his will if she continued gambling. I figure that's why she stopped.'

'And do you know anything about this guy she's been going around with lately?'

He shrugged. 'I'm afraid I can't help you there. He may have come in here but

I don't ask the names of any customers who come to play the tables. So long as they don't make any trouble they can come in at any time.'

I stubbed out my cigarette. I wasn't getting anywhere as far as this mysterious stranger was concerned. No one appeared to have seen him and even the detective Baker knew nothing about him. I'd followed all the leads I had and all of them led down a blind alley with a brick wall at the end of it.

'Thanks, Sam,' I said, getting to my feet. If she does happen to come in here with some guy I'd appreciate it if you'd let me know.'

'Just so long as you don't start any trouble in here that's fine by me.'

'I won't. All I want to do is find out who he is and what his relation is with Barbara Minton.'

Leaving the Golden Flamingo we went back to Dawn's apartment. At that moment I didn't want to think about anything except for a good night's sleep. Dawn switched on the electric fire and then poured a drink for both of us. I sipped mine slowly. It tasted good and slid down my throat like velvet. I'd half finished it when the phone rang.

Glancing down at my watch I looked across at Dawn. Very few, if any of my usual clients knew her number and it seemed a funny hour for anyone to be calling.

Dawn picked up the receiver and held it to her ear. After listening for a moment, her face growing more apprehensive with each passing second, she held the phone out to me.

'Who is it?' I asked covering the mouthpiece with my hand.

'It's some man. He says he knows you're here and wants to speak to you.'

'Merak,' I said harshly.

'I hear you've been asking questions about Barbara Minton,' said a voice I didn't recognize. 'That isn't very wise.'

'Who the hell is this?' I demanded. 'I don't like people phoning me without giving their names.'

'Never mind who I am. All you need to know is that I'm a very good friend of Barbara's and you seem to be pushing your nose into things that don't concern you.'

'I'm afraid that's my business, friend, finding out things some people don't want me to know,' I retorted. 'Unless I know exactly to whom I'm talking I don't think we have anything more to say.'

'I'm simply trying to give you a warning. This is for your own good. Either lay off Mrs. Minton or I won't be responsible for the consequences.'

'You won't be responsible! Listen buster, I don't take kindly to threats from anyone, particularly folk who daren't give their names. But if you're the guy who met up with Barbara Minton this morning on the freeway I guess you should know the cops are on the lookout for you.'

There was a derisive laugh on the other end of the line. 'The cops don't worry me. But you're a little too persistent for my liking. Just stay out of this or you'll regret it.'

I made to say something more but there was a click on the end of the line and the phone went dead. I put the receiver down.

'I gather that was someone you don't know,' Dawn remarked.

'Whoever he was he refused to give his name but my guess is he's the one we're looking for.'

'What exactly did he want?'

'He's getting a trifle worried and tried to warn me to get off that case.'

Getting to her feet she said softly, 'My advice is to sleep on it, Johnny. You might see things a little more clearly in the morning.'

I knew she was right. My mind was too full of different things at the moment. I needed to clear it of the dross and concentrate on the more important information.

* * *

The following morning I woke to find it was almost sunrise. Dawn was already awake and in the kitchen preparing something to eat. There was the smell of hot coffee and frying bacon in the air as I walked through.

'Feeling better?' she asked, glancing at

me over her shoulder.

'A lot,' I replied, seating myself at the table. 'I've been trying to figure things out and I reckon I'll try to find this guy Cortega and have a talk with him.'

Dawn turned sharply at that. 'Don't you think that could be dangerous, Johnny?'

'That's true. But I'm not going to get anywhere without asking questions.'

Once breakfast was over I went outside to where the Merc was parked after telling Dawn to ask around the downtown quarter and check if there was any evidence of a protection racket being run in the vicinity.

It wasn't until I slid behind the wheel of the car that I realized I had no idea where Cortega might hang out. I finally decided to check with some of the local bars in the area. The guys who ran these often knew most of what was going on in their territory. The trouble was — would they talk to me?

The first three I tried were local dives. I asked a few discreet questions but either no one knew Cortega — or if they did they weren't talking. Quite often it wasn't wise to talk about killers like Cortega, especially to strangers who might be either undercover cops or working for some other outfit.

The fourth one I went into also looked as though it had seen better days. There were few customers, which didn't really surprise me from the look of the place. The amount of cigarette ash on the floor was almost enough to make a grey carpet in front of the counter. There was a solitary bulb suspended from the ceiling but for all the light it gave it was totally superfluous. A couple of the guys seated at the tables turned to glance at me and then went back to staring down at their drink. From their attitude I guessed that few strangers ever frequented the joint. Those who did would usually leave after their first drink. It wasn't the sort of place in which to spend even a short summer vacation.

I walked up to the bar and signalled to the bartender. His whole attitude was one of suspicion. I figured he wasn't sure whether I was a cop or a member of the

Organization. Whichever he reckoned I might be, I certainly wasn't welcome there.

'What'll it be, mister?' he grunted finally. He probably thought that if I got a drink I might leave.

'Bourbon, straight,' I said.

When he brought it, I asked in a low voice, 'You know where I can find Vinnie Cortega?'

His fleshy features remained completely blank. 'Sorry friend, I've never heard the name.'

I took a ten-spot from my wallet and held it out in front of him. His eyes lit up at that, his gaze following my hand as if mesmerized as I placed it on the counter in front of him. Taking out another ten-dollar bill I laid it on top of the other.

I expected him to try to snatch the dough but instead he asked, 'Why do you want to see him, mister? Believe me, he's poison.'

'So I've heard. But it's important I find him.'

'Are you a cop?'

'I'm a private detective investigating a

disappearance,' I told him. I took out my business card and gave it to him. He squinted at it shortsightedly before handing it back.

Straightening up he threw a swift glance around the room and then leaned forward so that his face almost touched mine. 'You won't live long, mister, asking questions like that around these parts.'

'I'll worry about that. Just tell me where I can find him.'

The barkeep ran his tongue around lips that had suddenly gone dry. Then he muttered: 'He usually frequents the Golden Nugget off Fifth Street. Just remember. You haven't heard this from me.'

'Heard what?' I said.

His hand went down and the dough disappeared like magic beneath his fleshy fingers. A second later it had vanished into his pocket.

Turning, I left. He was still staring after me as I reached the door, scratching his head with a worried expression on his face. I guessed he was wondering whether he'd done the right thing or not. It seemed that this hoodlum Cortega had some kind of hold over most people in this part of town.

I could guess, from the time I'd spent working for the Organization, how he did it. Fear was the driving factor. He'd get together a small outfit made up of killers who carried out every order he gave and anyone who stepped out of line would disappear with no questions asked. It was the way in which every outfit in the Underworld worked and it paid off dividends every time.

Unlike the places I'd just left, the Golden Nugget was a real classy joint, the kind most of the Big Boys used as a meeting place. Parking my car on the opposite side of the street I gave it the once-over. I could guess at the setup. Nobody got past the two guys at the door unless they were well known or especially invited. Taking a chance I walked right up to them.

'Is Vinnie Cortega in?'

Both of them eyed me as if I was a little touched in the head asking such a question. Then one of them said, 'You a friend of Vinnie's?' His voice was like gravel rumbling down a chute.

'I'd like to be,' I replied innocently. 'If he is on the premises I'd like to speak to him on an urgent matter.'

'And who told you he might be here?' queried the other guy. His voice sounded just the same as his companion's.

'A mutual friend,' I said. I was getting nowhere. I had the feeling these guys would keep on asking questions until I got tired and went away.

Just at that moment, however, this guy approached from somewhere inside. He looked sharply at me through the small gap between the two bruisers. Evidently he'd overheard our conversation for he said quietly, 'You asking about Vinnie Cortega, friend?'

'That's right,' I told him.

Giving a quick jerk of his head, he said, 'All right, boys, I'll take care of this.' To me, he went on, 'Then I guess you'd better come inside and speak your piece.'

The two doormen stepped aside and I brushed past them. I'd somehow got inside the place but there was a nagging suspicion in my mind that it might not be so easy getting out.

Pausing at the bar, the guy with me motioned to the bartender who was standing behind the counter doing nothing. 'Get a drink for my friend here, Al, and bring it through into the back room.'

In reply to the other's inquiring look, I said, 'Bourbon on the rocks will be fine.'

My companion took me firmly by the arm and led me towards the door at the far side of the room. Lifting his free hand he knocked twice; then pushed the door open and nudged me inside. The room was bigger than I'd expected. Three men were inside, one of them sitting apart from the other two and I guessed he was the man I was looking for.

Classily dressed, he had the dark hair indicative of his Sicilian heritage. A small moustache gave him a somewhat distinguished appearance but it was his eyes, like those of a snake about to strike, that gave him away as a killer who would shoot first and then ask questions.

They all looked up as the guy with me

said, 'This punk was asking a lot of questions, Vinnie. He says he wants to see you about something important.'

'Has he been frisked for a weapon?' Cortega had spotted the bulge beneath my left arm.

For a moment, the guy with me didn't know what to say. He'd obviously made a big mistake taking me in there without relieving me of any artillery I was carrying. It was a mistake he'd doubtless regret in the near future.

I took out the .38 very carefully and placed it on the table. I didn't want any of them getting the wrong impression. 'I guess he just forgot,' I said. 'I didn't come here to kill anyone, just to ask a few questions.'

At that moment there was a knock on the door and the barkeep came in with my drink. He put it down on the table in front of the empty chair.

Cortega leaned back in his chair and motioned me to sit down. Turning to the guy who'd brought me, he said, 'I'll see you later.' The look in his eyes told me that my friend was in big trouble.

'All right, so you want to ask questions,' Cortega placed both hands on the table. 'Who are you, an undercover cop — or one of the other outfits?'

'Neither,' I told him. I took out my card and slid it across the table.

Picking it up, he glanced down at it and then pushed it back. Turning, he eyed each of the other two men in turn. 'His name is Johnny Merak, boys. A Private Investigator.' Swinging his gaze back to me, he went on, 'So what would a private dick want with me?'

From the way he asked the question I knew I was treading on dangerous ground. If he once got the idea I was pushing my nose into his business my hopes of getting out of this place in one piece were rapidly fading over the horizon.

Choosing my words carefully, I said, 'I'm investigating the disappearance of a woman named Barbara Minton. Her car was found on the Orange Freeway yesterday morning, completely burnt-out. However, there was no sign of her. My guess is that she either ran off with another man or she was forcibly abducted.'

'So why should that be of any interest to me? I've never even heard of the dame.'

'Does the name Baker mean anything to you — James Baker?'

I noticed the little flicker in his eyes at my mention of the name. There was a slight hesitation before he answered. 'He's also some kind of private eye, ain't he?'

'He was until yesterday. He was found in his office with a bullet through his head.'

That made him jerk forward in his chair. 'Murder?'

I nodded. 'That's right. How well did you know him?'

I didn't expect him to answer me — but he did. 'O.K. I don't know how you worked it out but he was doing a job for me. I've got a nice little business here and I intend to make it even bigger. But someone has been cutting in on me. A couple of my places have been torched and two of my boys killed. I hired him to find out who's behind it.' His features sharpened. 'Are you looking to take over his job? So far he's discovered nothing for me. Maybe you'd be better than he was.'

'I've already been hired by Edward Minton to continue Baker's work and at the moment it means I've two really important cases on my hands,' I told him. 'I'm afraid I wouldn't have time for any more.'

He looked disappointed and angry. Very softly, he said, 'I'm not used to being turned down, Merak. On this occasion I think you should reconsider your decision.' There was a definite note of menace now in his voice.

I knew I was treading on dangerous ground now. Hoping to stall him for a little while, I asked, 'May I ask if you'd be prepared to tell me everything, if I were to agree to your request? I can assure you that anything you tell me is strictly confidential between you and me. No one will hear about it from me.'

'Not even Minton or the cops?'

'No one,' I assured him.

He pressed his thin lips into a straight, hard line, turning that over in his mind.

Then he nodded. 'O.K. I'll go along with that.' Turning to the two guys sitting like statues in their chairs, he said sharply, 'Take a hike, boys. And see that I'm not disturbed.'

Once they had gone, closing the door quietly behind them, he leaned forward, placing the tips of his fingers together. Surveying me over the fleshy pyramid, he went on, 'I don't know how good a detective you are, Merak, but I guess I'll have to trust you. I may be able to help you with these other cases you have but none of it goes beyond these four walls. And I'm warning you — cross me and you're finished, permanently. You got that?'

'I've got it. What is it you want me to do?' I certainly didn't want to take on anything for him but when it came to a choice between that and lying on a mortuary slab there was nothing else I could do. There was an ashtray on the table and, leaning back, I lit a cigarette, hoping it would calm my nerves. Those little mice running around inside my head were telling me I'd been a fool to come into this place. With an effort, I tried to ignore them.

'When I told you earlier that I'd never heard of Barbara Minton it wasn't the truth. Far from it as a matter of fact. But I reckon you've already guessed that.'

Blowing smoke into the air, I took a swallow of my drink. 'I figured you might be lying,' I admitted. 'So how well did you know her?'

His lips curled into what was meant to be a smile. 'You don't have to look any further. I'm the one who's been seeing her behind her husband's back.'

I felt a sudden sense of shock. This was the last thing I'd expected to hear. I knew he was telling the truth. He would never have admitted it to me otherwise. 'And how long has this affair been going on? According to what I've been told you've only just arrived in L.A.'

'I've known her for more than three years. We met in a nightclub in Mexico City and hit it off almost at once. After our first meeting she used to drive over the border quite often on the pretext of meeting an old friend of hers.'

'And her husband never suspected anything?'

'Not at first. Then, of course, he hired this private dick James Baker. That's when I decided to hire him as well to make sure he never found out anything to link me with her.'

'Did you kill him to make absolutely certain he never discovered anything?' His eyes narrowed to mere slits at that remark and I went on hurriedly. 'You understand I have to ask these questions.'

Shrugging, he went on, 'Why should I kill him? He gave me every bit of information I needed to know exactly what her husband was doing. Minton may have thought that Baker was working exclusively for him. In reality, he was doing everything I told him.'

I tried to put the riot of thoughts in my mind into some kind of logical order. Cortega's admission certainly solved one problem for me. But there were a lot of other questions to which I needed answers if I was to make any progress. I decided to push on now I'd got his attention.

'Then you were the guy who met her yesterday out on the freeway. The two of you set fire to her car, hoping to disappear together?'

'That's right. It was all arranged between us some days earlier.'

'I see. Then perhaps you can tell me where she is now.'

He shook his head at that. 'I'd tell you if I knew — but unfortunately I don't.'

'I don't understand. Evidently you left the scene of the fire together. What happened after that?'

'Are all these questions absolutely necessary? I'm just hiring you to find out who's trying to destroy my business. What has Barbara Minton got to do with that?'

I couldn't answer that and I didn't want him getting too suspicious or he might decide I was getting too nosy and decide he didn't need me after all. Thinking on my feet, I said, 'There's just the chance that Minton knows you're the one his wife has been seeing and he's behind these attacks on your property. The longer his wife isn't found, the more difficult it's going to be to prove that.'

He ran that thought over in his mind, then nodded briefly. 'All right. I drove her into town. She asked me to drop her off at the corner of Fifth and Main, saying she'd get in touch with me in a couple of hours. That was the last I saw of her.'

Picking up the glass I finished my drink. 'You've been very helpful, Mister Cortega,' I said, getting to my feet. 'I'll be in touch with you as soon as I have anything.'

'What do you intend to do now?'

'The important thing, of course, is to find Barbara Minton — but since she seems determined to stay out of sight that isn't going to be easy. In the meantime I'll have another word with her husband. If she should contact you again I'd be grateful if you'd let me know. As far as I'm aware she's done nothing illegal but there are some questions I'd like answered.'

'I'll do that,' Cortega got up and opened the door for me. Picking up the .38 from the desk I thrust it back into the shoulder holster. The two guys I'd seen earlier were standing there like Gog and

Magog. Cortega said something to one of them in a low voice. Taking my arm, the guy led me to the street door.

'Just one more thing, Mister Cortega,' I said, pausing between the two bruisers. 'Did you phone my secretary's number a little while ago and warn me off the Barbara Minton case?'

He looked puzzled. 'No, I've phoned no one today. I don't have your secretary's number.'

I pushed past the big guys onto the sidewalk. The fresh air tasted good after the atmosphere inside the Golden Nugget. I told myself I was lucky to be alive after that conversation with Cortega. At least he had cleared up one point that had been worrying me. Now I knew the identity of the guy who was having the affair with Barbara Minton.

Not that it did me much good. As I got behind the wheel of the Merc I tried to figure out just why he had been so willing to impart that information. Cortega was clearly one of those guys who had a reason for everything they did. Nothing came into my mind so I decided to leave that problem for later.

Back at the office I found Dawn waiting for me. 'Did you find this man Cortega?' she asked as I sat down.

I nodded. I finally found him but it took a little time. I also managed to have quite a long talk with him.'

She looked surprised. 'And you still came out of it without any trouble?' She put the kettle on and spooned coffee into a couple of mugs.

Leaning back, I said, 'Not only that but he seemed quite willing to talk provided I accepted a case for him.'

She was silent until she brought the coffee over and then sat down in the other chair opposite me. 'Did you accept? Surely you've got enough work on without doing anything for this killer.'

Sipping the hot coffee, I said, 'You don't know these guys as I do, Dawn. You either do as they ask or you end up in the ocean with lead in your pockets. However, apart from that he seemed quite willing to talk and what he told me I reckon was the truth. One little problem has been solved for us.'

She arched her eyebrows at that. 'Something important?'

'Very. He's the guy who's been seeing Barbara Minton. He was with her yesterday morning and the two of them set fire to her car. Then he drove her into L.A.'

'So he knows where she is now?'

'Unfortunately, he doesn't. At least, that's what he claims. He left her at the corner of Fifth and Main after arranging to see her again that day. She never turned up and he can't get in touch with her. My guess is that she was using him for her own ends and now she could be anywhere — if she's still alive.'

'So we're no closer to finding her?'

Shaking my head, I drank down the rest of the coffee. It burned my throat but it cleared my brain. 'Did you find out anything more about him?'

Going back to her desk, she picked up her notebook and brought it over, flipping through the pages. 'As you'd expect, there isn't much. There's a lot of hearsay but not many concrete facts. It's apparently quite true that he's extorting money from a lot of people in return for protection. Any who don't pay up have their premises smashed by his heavies and are physically beaten up.'

'However, there are rumours that someone is out to get him. A few of his own places have been set on fire and some of his own men have been found dead at various locations throughout the city. So far the police are treating this as some kind of gang war between rival outfits. They don't seem to be doing much about it.'

'It almost certainly is a gang war,' I agreed. 'He told me that himself and that's why he wants me to find out who is starting this vendetta against him.'

'You're a goddamn fool if you do, Johnny,' she sighed. 'But knowing you as I do, you'll take the case in spite of the fact that Manzelli warned you against it.'

'Manzelli!' I sat up straight. 'I'd almost forgotten about him. So we now have two of the Organization having death threats made against them. That's very interesting.'

'Why? You surely don't think that the

same person is responsible for these threats? There's nothing definite to connect Manzelli and Cortega.'

'Perhaps not. But if there is and we discover what it is, we've got the one responsible.'

3

The Man in the shadows

It was two days later before I got anything like a break. Dawn checked as far as possible into Barbara Minton and her associations with various men since her marriage but seemed to be getting nowhere. If anything was going on, both Lieutenant Morgan and O'Leary were keeping it under their hats. Barbara Minton appeared to have vanished off the face of the Earth but since I didn't believe in alien abductions I felt sure that, if she were still alive, she'd gone to ground someplace.

I was sitting in my chair reading through Baker's notes for the second time when the phone rang. It had an urgent note to it. Picking up the receiver, I said, 'Merak.'

It was Lieutenant O'Leary's clipped tones and he didn't sound too pleased.

'We've got a body on our hands, Merak. I'd like you here. You may be able to identify it for me.'

'Where are you, Lieutenant?' I asked.

'On the waterfront not far from the harbour.'

'I'll be there in fifteen minutes,' I told him. I put down the phone.

As I made my way down to the street I tried to figure out why he thought I might be able to identify the stiff. O'Leary knew most of the crooks and hoodlums by sight. So how come he didn't know who it was. The only conclusion I could reach was that Barbara Minton had finally been found. It was possible O'Leary didn't know her by sight whereas I did have a photograph of her provided by her husband.

I gunned the Merc across town towards the waterfront. While still fifty yards from the spot, I picked out the small group of men standing down at the water's edge. O'Leary glanced up as I approached. There was a body lying face down on the sand where it had obviously been dragged out of the sea.

'Thanks for coming,' the Lieutenant muttered. It wasn't often he thanked anyone so he was either feeling out of his depth or, less likely, he really meant it. Going down on one knee I took a close look at the body. Since it wasn't a woman I was able to put Barbara Minton out of my mind.

Glancing up at O'Leary I asked, 'Do you mind if I turn him over, Lieutenant?'

'We haven't got any pictures yet but I guess it's O.K.'

Grasping the guy's shoulder I pulled him over onto his back. Little fingers of ice began brushing along my spine as I stared down into the face of Vinnie Cortega! There was a nasty looking hole in the back of his head.

Staring across the body at O'Leary, I said harshly, 'Sure I recognize him but he wasn't drowned. Somebody put a slug into the back of his skull before he was tossed into the ocean.'

'I can see that,' O'Leary snapped. 'But do you know who he is?'

'Yes, I know him. I was talking to him only a couple of days ago. His name is

Vinnie Cortega. A small time crook who's only recently come to L.A. He ran a protection racket in the downtown area. He was hoping to hit the big time but without letting any of the other outfits know.'

There was a hard, suspicious glint in the other's eyes as he said thinly, 'All right. Now suppose you tell me just how you came to be having a cosy little chat with him.'

I hesitated; then figured that now he was obviously dead there was no point in holding anything back from the cops.

Straightening up I said, 'I wanted to get the answers. There were some questions I had about the Minton woman.'

O'Leary's forehead furrowed as he digested that. Finally, he asked tersely, 'What possible connection could there be between him and Barbara Minton?'

'Perhaps I should be telling this to Lieutenant Morgan but — '

'Never mind about Morgan.' O'Leary almost snarled the words. 'You'll tell me — now. I'll let him know if I think it's important.'

'Fair enough. From what I saw at the scene of that car fire, I knew someone had met her there and then gone off with her. I wasn't sure about him but I had the feeling he knew something more about it than he was telling. Finally he admitted that he'd known her for three years. They first met in Mexico and he was secretly having an affair with her behind her husband's back.'

'He was taking a chance admitting that to you, wasn't he?'

'Perhaps. But he wanted me to do something for him and he knew I'd either keep my mouth shut or risk a dip in the sea all the way to the bottom.'

Running a finger down his cheek, O'Leary glanced down at the body at his feet. He seemed to believe me but his suspicious nature was still well to the fore. 'O.K. I guess you're telling the truth. Now suppose you tell me what you were to do for him in return for this information. And don't give me any of this client confidentiality crap.'

'Sure. He's dead now so I reckon it won't matter much to him. Someone was sending him threatening letters. Whoever it was, they were backing up the threats by killing a number of his boys and burning down some of his property.'

'And you agreed to help him find out who this other killer is?'

'That's right.'

'One of these days, Merak, you're going to finish up on a slab yourself. Why the hell don't you stick to finding missing husbands? Leave the homicides to us. That way you're going to live a lot longer.'

He stalked off to where a couple of cops were standing looking bored. I went back down on my knees and examined Cortega's body more closely. There was no sign of any powder burns around the wound. Clearly he'd been shot from a distance and whoever had done it was an excellent shot. I wondered what would happen to his protection racket now he was dead.

Those little mice were still cartwheeling through my mind coming up with a host of questions to which there were, as yet, no answers. This could have been a gang killing — someone in his outfit wanted him out of the way so they could take over. It happened quite often and it was something that would be of interest to Manzelli — if he didn't already know about it. From the manner in which this slaying had been carried out it bore all the hallmarks of a mob execution. And there were quite a few of the Big Boys, apart from Manzelli, who didn't like the idea of him starting anything without consulting the Organization. Obviously he'd been shot before being dumped in the sea but why had he been taken out there and dropped overboard?

A thorough search told me his pockets were all empty so putting him into the water hadn't been done to hide the body. With nothing to take him to the bottom and keep the body there, the tide would wash him ashore pretty quickly. I turned all of these factors over in my mind before reaching another possible conclusion. There was, of course, someone else who might want Cortega dead — Edward Minton!

By now it was a near certainty that he'd

guessed the identity of the man his wife had been seeing. A moment's reflection told me that the flaw in that idea was that Minton was no professional killer. It was unlikely he'd carry out this murder by himself. So unless he'd paid some hitman to carry out the murder I couldn't see him being responsible.

O'Leary came back with one of the cops trailing at his heels. 'Have you seen everything you want, Merak?' he asked tersely.

I nodded. 'As much as is lying here,' I affirmed. 'But there's still a lot of it that doesn't make sense.'

'Well it looks like a clear-cut job to me. You say someone was out to kill him. Somehow this guy was able to get past any guards he had around and plug him in the back of the head. Then they took him a few miles out to sea and dropped him into the water. What's so mysterious about that?'

'If you just used your brains, Lieutenant, you'd know what it is. Why go to all that trouble? My guess is that he was killed someplace else and then brought here. If it was to make certain his body wasn't discovered they'd have weighed it down — but they didn't. So they must have known the tide would wash him ashore in a very short time.'

I paused as another thought struck me. 'Do you have any idea how long he's been dead?'

O'Leary shook his head. 'Offhand I'd say just a few hours but we'll have to wait for the autopsy to get an accurate figure.'

'Would you let me know when you hear from the medical boys?'

'All right. Why — do you reckon it's important?'

'I'm not sure. It might explain some of the doubts I've got about this case.'

'O'Leary looked up sharply. 'This isn't your case, Merak. This is purely a homicide matter.'

'Not at all. Cortega asked me to find out who was responsible for the threatening letters he was getting and also who was eliminating some of his boys. As far as I'm concerned, I'm still on the case.'

He didn't like that. I thought he was about to warn me off it but instead he spun on his heel and stormed off back to where a couple of other guys had arrived on the scene.

I decided it was time to leave. There was nothing more I wanted to see and I figured I'd leave O'Leary to his own devices. Back at the office I told Dawn what had happened. She listened intently until I'd finished and then said, with a puzzled frown. 'Does the Lieutenant have any clues as to the identity of the killer?'

'None at all. But like me, he can't understand why anyone shot Cortega and then went to all the trouble of dumping his body into the bay without weighing it down so that it stayed there.'

She thought that over, clearly trying to find some plausible explanation. Then she shrugged.

'There's only one possibility I can think of.'

'What's that?' I asked.

'Suppose that after he'd been shot there was something on his skin or clothing that could be identified. The killer may have figured the sea would effectively wash it off.'

'If you're thinking of powder burns that's not the answer. Salt water wouldn't remove them.'

'I was thinking about perfume.'

'You think that whoever killed him was a woman who seduced him, hoping to lull him into a false sense of security before killing him and before he had a chance to realize what was happening? That's possible I guess. But that would put Barbara Minton right at the top of the list of suspects.'

The more I thought it over the more plausible it seemed. Cortega had told me that she'd broken her promise to meet him in a few hours. Maybe her true feelings towards him weren't quite as loving as she'd made out.

'I guess that's something we should look into,' I said finally, 'once we find her.'

'And that won't be easy especially if she has friends who're willing to hide her.'

At that moment, the phone rang. I guessed it might be Lieutenant Morgan, feeling a little peeved that he hadn't been informed about any connection between

Barbara Minton and Cortega — but it wasn't.

'That you, Merak?' It was O'Leary's voice.

'Sure,' I replied. 'There's not usually anyone else in my office apart from my secretary.'

'Don't try my patience, Merak. If I have to dig any further into this goddamned case I swear I'll be leaving here with the men in the white coats. I just phoned to tell you that the forensic boys have compared the slug that killed Cortega and the one that was taken from James Baker's skull.'

'And — ?'

'It seems they were both fired from the same gun.'

'That's impossible.' I experienced a sudden sense of shock at his words. 'Your boys are absolutely certain about this?'

'Absolutely. O.K. I know it doesn't make sense. That weapon was brought here to the precinct as police evidence. I brought it myself.'

'And where is it now?'

'I've just checked. It's locked away in the armoury.'

'And it's never been taken out since it was removed from Baker's office as evidence?'

There was a pause, then, 'Not to my knowledge.'

'Then we've got a real mystery on our hands.'

'Think it over and if you can come up with anything that makes sense, let me know.' O'Leary put the phone down. I knew he was as puzzled as I was.

Noticing the expression on my face, Dawn asked, 'You've got something on your mind, Johnny.'

The way she said it made it more of a statement than a question.

'Yeah. The bullet that just killed Cortega came from the same gun as Jim Baker had in his hand when he was found. The two slugs from both slayings are identical, proving the same weapon was used in both murders.'

Dawn began filing her nails. It was something she always did when she was trying to work something out. Then she looked up sharply. 'Then there's only one explanation.'

'If there is, I'd be glad to hear it because this news has got me stymied.'

'Don't you see? That bullet that killed Baker wasn't fired from his gun. The killer shot him with his own weapon, also a .45. After firing one shot from Baker's gun he placed it carefully in the detective's hand to make it look like suicide.'

'And he still had his own weapon with which to kill Cortega. So naturally both slugs came from the same weapon. Dawn, you're a genius. Sometimes, I think you should be doing my job. That has to be the answer. It should be easy enough to prove. All O'Leary has to do is fire a bullet from the weapon he's got stashed away in his armoury and compare it with the other two. If they're different that'll prove that Baker's gun wasn't used in either murder.'

I picked up the phone and dialled the Lieutenant's number. He answered straight away.

'You're not going mad, Lieutenant,' I said.

'What the hell do you mean by that?'

'Those two identical slugs,' I replied. 'My assistant has just figured out the answer. Neither of them came from the gun we found in Baker's hand and which you've now got safely locked away.'

He was silent for a long moment. I could picture him staring down at the telephone wondering if I'd just lost my marbles.

Briefly, I gave him the explanation Dawn had just put forward. He wasn't the brightest cop on the force and it took him a couple of minutes to get the explanation through his skull. But he got it in the end. 'She's right, of course. Why the hell didn't we think of that? Tell her if she wants a job in my department I'll back her for it.'

'It also tells us something else, Lieutenant. Something more important.'

'What's that?'

'Isn't it obvious? It means the same killer who shot Baker also murdered Cortega. Unfortunately it doesn't get us any closer to finding out who he is. At the moment I can't think of any connection between Baker and Cortega except that both Minton and Cortega hired Baker to get some information for them.'

Something like a long sigh sounded over the line. I guessed O'Leary was still unhappy. 'All right, Johnny. Thanks for sorting this for me anyway. But stay out of this Cortega business. Have you got that?'

'I've got it, Lieutenant.'

'Good.' The line went dead as he put the receiver down.

At least he'd used my first name, which was a good sign. Leaning back I ran over in my mind any possible suspects for Cortega's killing. There weren't many. Edward Minton was still a possibility and there might be some of the Big Boys who didn't like the way he'd pushed himself into the Organization's territory. It was just possible the killer might have given the order for him to be eliminated to protect his own position.

I'd just put the phone down but before I could tell Dawn what O'Leary had said, there came a knock at the door.

I called out, 'It's open. Come in.'

Leaning back, I straightened my tie to make myself a little more presentable. I wasn't expecting anyone but in my business you never know who might drop in.

My first thought when the woman came in, closing the door quietly behind her, was that it was Barbara Minton. But I soon realized I was wrong.

I guessed she was in her mid-sixties although the makeup she wore made her look younger. Blonde hair neatly waved, loaded with high-class jewelry, I figured she was someone with plenty of dough. She wasn't my usual type of client and from the way she looked around her, it seemed she was wondering whether she'd come to the right place.

I stood up, noticing Dawn's querying look as she gave the woman the once-over. There was a gold wedding ring on her finger and another with the largest diamond I'd ever seen.

'Please take a seat, Mrs — ?'

'Silworth,' she said, sitting down elegantly in the chair opposite me. 'Ophelia Sitworth.'

I tried to cover up my sense of surprise. 'Then you must be Barbara's mother. We spoke on the phone a couple of days ago concerning the private detective your son-in-law hired.'

'That is correct. I understand that my son-in-law has now hired you to obtain certain information concerning her.'

I lowered myself into my chair. I had the sudden feeling that there might be trouble on the way if she started asking questions about her daughter.

'He has,' I told her, choosing my words carefully.

'I also understand that she has unaccountably disappeared and you're trying to find her.'

'That's also true,' I admitted. 'But why have you come to see me? The police are very insistent that this is a possible homicide case although at the moment it's a missing persons case as far as they're concerned.'

She looked somewhat disappointed at that. I guessed the primary reason she had come to see me rather than the police was to get what information I had on whether her daughter was cheating on her husband and who with. Her next words proved me right.

'I've known for some time that Barbara was seeing someone behind Edward's back and I'm quite certain I know who it is. Some man named Cortega, an Italian she met in Mexico a few years ago.'

'Then if you already know that how can we help you?' Dawn spoke up for the first time.

Ophelia Silworth eyed Dawn up and down as if wondering where she fitted into the picture.

Quickly, I said, 'This is my assistant. We work together on all of my cases and anything you say here is completely confidential.'

'Very well. What I really want from you is the whereabouts of this money-grabbing gigolo. Like all of his kind I'm sure he'll have his price.'

'You were hoping to buy him off?' I asked.

She twisted her lips in a strange kind of smile. 'Oh, it won't be difficult with men like him. I've met several in my life. He'll take the money and you won't see his heels for the dust.'

Leaning back, I stared up at the ceiling for a moment. From what she was saying it was clear she knew nothing of Cortega's murder. Quite possibly the news hadn't hit the streets yet. Finally, watching her reaction closely, I said, 'I'm afraid you won't be able to buy Cortega off, Mrs. Silworth.'

'Oh? Why not?' It was impossible to analyze her expression. Maybe she was thinking I didn't reckon she had enough dough.

'He was shot only a few hours ago. The police found his body on the beach where it had been washed up by the tide.'

She took a couple of minutes to digest that; then said harshly, 'So someone finally had the guts to take him out to sea after putting a bullet into his head and push him over the side. I can't say I'm sorry to hear it. Now, perhaps, she'll forget all about him and come to her senses. She has a perfectly good husband. Perhaps she takes after her father.'

I waited for her to say something more.

When she didn't I said evenly, 'Now I've given you this information, Mrs. Silworth, you won't be requiring my services.'

'On the contrary, if my daughter is still missing I need someone to find her. I realize that Edward, her husband, has already hired you but for a different reason. He apparently just wanted you to find out who she was seeing. You've already done that.'

I nodded but said nothing. I could see where this conversation was leading and Mrs. Silworth looked like a woman who didn't take no for an answer.

'Find my daughter, Mister Merak. That's all I'm asking. I'll make it worth your while.'

'Very well,' I said as she got up and moved towards the door. 'I'll do my best.'

'Thank you.' Pausing, she opened her expensive bag and took out a slim envelope. 'Ten thousand dollars. If you need more just let me know and I'll see that you get it.'

As she reached the door, I said sharply. 'Just one more thing, Mrs. Silworth, before you go.'

'Yes?'

'How is your husband?'

She looked completely mystified. 'My husband's very well.' She replied. 'Why shouldn't he be?'

Shrugging, I said, 'Oh, it's nothing. Just a thought that occurred to me.'

'It's a very strange kind of thought.' she remarked. Opening the door, still with a puzzled frown on her features, she left.

When she had gone, the echo of her footsteps fading along the corridor, Dawn asked, 'What was all that about her husband, Johnny? You don't suspect him of having anything to do with this; do you?'

'Not at all. I'm just wondering why Barbara lied to everyone when she supposedly visited her father who was, according to her, very ill in Colorado. So where was she all that time and what was she doing? She certainly wasn't seeing Cortega because she'd already made arrangements to meet him somewhere along the Orange Freeway.'

I glanced down at my watch. It was almost time to lock up. 'I reckon we'll leave that until tomorrow,' I said.

I walked across the room to check that all of the drawers in the filing cabinet were locked while Dawn put everything she needed into her bag. Before I could reach the door, however, it was pushed open and this guy stepped inside. I recognized his type straight away. Broad-shouldered with mean eyes and a hard look about his granite-like features.

'I'm glad I caught you before you left, Merak,' he rumbled in a voice like a saw cutting through timber, 'it'll save me a lot of trouble looking for you.'

'You got a problem, friend?' I asked. Dawn stood rigid beside her desk looking scared. There was no doubt this guy meant trouble of some kind.

'I reckon the problem is all yours,' he grunted. I noticed he kept his right hand close to his left shoulder. 'Someone wants to see you — now.'

'And who might this someone be?' I didn't think it was Manzelli. He already knew what I was doing.

'You'll find that out once you get there.' He motioned towards the door.

'And my assistant? What do you intend doing with her?'

My visitor threw a quick glance in Dawn's direction. 'I was told just to bring you. There was no mention of any dame.'

'All right. I'll see your boss — whoever he is.' I took my hat down from the peg. As I went out with the bruiser close behind me, I said over my shoulder, 'Everything's O.K. Dawn. Just finish locking up and go back to your apartment. I'll see you there in an hour or so.' I tried to speak more confidently than I felt. When one of the Big Boys asked to see you, it was impossible to be certain you'd ever come back.

I went out, leaving Dawn staring at me, a worried expression on her face. There was the usual large black limousine standing beside the sidewalk. Getting into the back, I suddenly realized my companion hadn't taken my gun. That was a good sign. Maybe this big shot just wanted to talk. If that was the case it was O.K. by me.

Closing the door behind him as he crushed in beside me, the bruiser said

114

something to the driver and we moved off through the early evening traffic. The journey took less than twenty minutes and when we finally came to a halt, I recognized the place at once and knew who I was going to meet. Sam Rizzio, head of perhaps the largest outfit in L.A.

The usual two guys were standing just inside the gates when we arrived. Opening them, we drove up to the font of Rizzio's mansion, set well back from the road. This time the normal routine was carried out and my .38 was taken from me the moment I got out of the car. Once inside the place I was taken to a room at the end of the long corridor.

Thrusting open the door, my guide motioned me to go in. Rizzio was seated behind the large desk on the far side of the room. There was a single empty chair in front of it and he motioned me to sit down with a negligent wave of his hand.

Placing his hands flat on the desk, he said softly, 'I thought it was time we had a talk, Johnny. It's been some time since we last met and certain events have happened which require urgent attention.'

'What events are those?' I asked. I'd known Rizzio for some years and so far our meetings had been cordial. At the moment, I wanted them to continue that way. My position, however, was still precarious. One word he didn't like and I might not see tomorrow.

'This punk who tried to muscle in on the Organization — Cortega for instance.'

'He's dead,' I said.

Rizzio smiled but there was no mirth in it. 'I know that. But who can be sure that someone in his outfit isn't about to take over where he left off? If that should happen it could be most unfortunate.'

He sat back and regarded me closely. After a momentary pause, he went on, 'I've also heard whispers that you were working for him, Johnny. What was that all about?'

I knew better than to lie to him. With the single exception of Manzelli, he probably knew more of what went on in the Los Angeles Underworld than anyone else.

'He was apparently involved with Barbara Minton. She disappeared from a burnt-out car on the Orange freeway. It seems he was with her at the time she vanished. After he brought her back to L.A. she promised to meet him later that day and when she didn't turn up he asked me to find her. That's all there was to it.'

'And do you have any idea who killed him?'

'I've no idea at all.' From the expression on his angular features it was impossible to tell whether or not he believed me.

Then he suddenly switched the subject. 'Have you received any word from Manzelli recently?'

'Manzelli!' I wondered if, by some means, he'd discovered that the Big Boss had been to see me. I tried to look suitably surprised. 'Why the hell would he want to see me?'

'Just a thought, Johnny. I've heard rumours that he's received more threatening notes. If there's any truth in them I reckon you'd be the first he'd approach to discover who's sending them.'

'So far I've heard nothing from him,' I said, trying to keep my voice steady.

Inwardly, I felt as if I were driving a twenty-ton truck over very thin ice. 'Whenever he wants to see me he always sends a couple of his boys along. There've been rumours like that several times. That's all this is — just a rumour.'

He stared up at the ceiling as if seeing something of great importance written there, then dropped his gaze. 'All right, Johnny. I guess that's all for now.'

I got up. The big bruiser was still standing at the door. Before he opened it, I turned back to Rizzio. 'There's just one question I'd like to ask you, Sam.'

His eyebrows went up until they almost disappeared into his hair. 'What's that?'

'Do you, or any of your boys, know anything about this dame, Barbara Minton? It seems she's still missing.'

'I know nothing about her and I'm sure none of my boys do either. We don't mess with dames like that. They can be trouble, big trouble.'

'Thanks.' I turned and followed my guide outside where my gun was returned to me. I got into the car waiting at the entrance and settled back in the seat. This time there was no one else in the car apart from the driver and myself. He never said a word so obviously he'd already been given his orders. A quarter of an hour we arrived in front of the office building.

My car was still where I'd left it and I was on the point of opening the door when I noticed something strange. The light inside the office was still on! Those little mice inside my mind woke up at that. They were telling me that Dawn was not the kind of woman to forget to switch the light off when she locked up the place. I went inside the building making as little noise as possible. Taking out the .38 I made my way up the stairs. Slowly, I edged my way along the corridor. Reaching, the office door I tried the handle. It was unlocked. Now things were beginning to look sinister.

Twisting the handle, I thrust the door open and stepped inside. At first I could see very little out of order. Then I spotted the pair of legs protruding from behind my desk. Running forward, I found Dawn lying on the floor. She had her hands tied behind her back, there was a length of rope around her slim ankles and a gag thrust into her mouth.

It was the work of a couple of minutes to free her and help her to a chair. 'What the hell happened, Dawn?' I asked.

Swallowing thickly, she managed to get words out. 'You'd only just left with that man, Johnny. I'd just put the key into the door when these two guys popped up out of nowhere. Both had guns in their hands. The next thing I knew one of them hit me on the side of my head with a gun butt. I guess I must have passed out for a few minutes because when I came round I'd been tied up and gagged and dumped where you found me. They were going through the files in the cabinet, obviously looking for something.'

Going back to my desk I took out the half-empty bottle of Scotch and poured a generous measure into a glass. She took it from me and I noticed that her hand was shaking. The glass rattled against her teeth as she took a couple of swallows.

After a few moments, she'd pulled herself together. 'Who do you reckon they were, Johnny? What were they looking for?'

I poured myself a drink. 'I can guess who they were — Rizzio's boys. He's the only one who'd know this office was likely to be empty once he'd got me over to his place. I thought it was funny at the time.'

'Funny?' Dawn asked, eyeing me over the rim of her glass.

'It was quite clear he hadn't had me taken there to talk about anything important. He already knew that Cortega was dead. What else was there for him to know? As to what those men were looking for — did you notice if they took any papers when they left?'

She shook her head. 'I couldn't see much from where they'd put me, I'm afraid.'

Leaving my drink on the desk I walked over to the filing cabinet and riffled through the contents. As far as I could tell everything was still there. Then I noticed that something was missing. The notes that had belonged to Jim Baker concerning the cases he was working on. Pushing the drawer back, I tried the key in the lock. It still worked. Whoever had picked the lock was certainly an expert at his job.

Dawn finished her drink and then got slowly to her feet. She held on to the edge of the desk for a moment.

'Are you feeling all right now?' I asked anxiously. 'That must have been quite a blow you got.'

'I'm fine, she nodded.'

'Perhaps you should stay at my place tonight,' I said. 'I've got enough food in to rustle up a meal for us.'

'I'd like that,' she replied. She was like that — always saying the right thing.

We drove back to my apartment and while I prepared something to eat I gave her another drink. We spoke little while we ate but once we were finished, she said, 'What was it those men took, Johnny? Anything important?'

'All they got were Baker's case notes. Rizzio must have guessed they'd end up with me once the cops had finished with them. The way I see it, Rizzio's somehow in with Edward Minton. We know Minton's well in with Manzelli and probably several other bosses too.'

'But what's his game?'

'That's something I don't know. But there's a little suspicion in my mind that, in spite of all the outward appearances, his wife is the one with the money. If that's the case he'll do everything in his power to keep her, even if it means turning a blind eye to any extra-marital affairs she might have.'

I stretched out my legs and tried to relax. Dawn pursed her lips I had the feeling she didn't go along with that idea.

After a few moments, she said, 'There's something else we have to take into consideration. He can't divorce her or let her divorce him because then he'd get nothing. But if he was to — '

'Arrange for an accident to happen to her — or a murder,' I finished. 'That way he'd get everything. Certainly the Mobs have their methods of getting rid of unwanted people. That could be what he's planning with someone in the Organization.'

Dawn nodded. 'And since she's disappeared it may already be too late.'

I turned that idea over in my mind. It

certainly fitted most of the facts we had. There were, of course, a few bits of the jigsaw that didn't fall into place. For instance, I couldn't see any reason why Edward Minton would send any threatening notes to Manzelli. I decided to leave it all until the next day.

There was someone out there in the shadows and whoever he was, he was extremely clever at covering his tracks.

4

Find The Lady

A couple of days passed and I was still getting nowhere. I knew Manzelli would soon be getting impatient and would start asking awkward questions. If he figured I might be either stalling or spending too much time on searching for Barbara Minton he might decide I was no longer any use to him and that could be fatal where Johnny Merak was concerned.

Just to keep tabs on what was happening with Cortega's outfit now that he'd vacated this earthly life I sent Dawn to ask around again in the downtown quarter. If someone had taken over from him and was still running the show I wanted to know. The trouble was, it would be bad news.

I'd already come to the conclusion that Barbara Minton was still alive. If she'd been killed in the same manner as her former lover I felt sure her body would have been found someplace. Whoever was carrying out these murders would have no reason to hide the body. It would be dumped someplace like Cortega's waiting for someone to stumble over it.

That could only mean that she was either being concealed somewhere against her will or, for some reason known only to herself, she was keeping out of sight of the general population. L.A. was a big place. There were plenty of places where she could be. I told myself if I had to start somewhere it would be well off the beaten track in one of the abandoned areas of the city.

Ten minutes later I drove out towards the waterfront. Here there were long rows of warehouses and wooden jetties. I had a recent photograph of Barbara Minton in my jacket pocket but I didn't figure on meeting many folk to ask if they'd seen her. No one who came to L.A. for a visit ever came to places like this unless they were on the run from the law and needed a hideout. It wouldn't have looked out of place if someone had taken it and dropped it in the middle of the desert.

Stopping the Merc, I got out and looked around me. My first impression was that the place was totally abandoned. The usual rodent population would be somewhere around in the dark shadows but that was the only sign of life there'd be. Then I picked up the sound of approaching automobiles and a few seconds later three cars appeared around the corner at the far end of the street. They were police cars and, watching them approach, I wondered what the cops were after in this dump.

They pulled up close to the Merc. The big guy who came towards me looked familiar but for a moment I couldn't place him. Then I recognized him. Lieutenant Morgan.

'I certainly didn't expect to find you here, Mister Merak,' he said genially. 'unless you're carrying out a search for the same person as I am.'

'Barbara Minton?'

He nodded. 'That's right. We've been combing most of the deserted areas like this but so far without any success.' He turned abruptly and signalled to the men with him to spread out and check all of the buildings. 'Watch your step, men,' he called loudly, 'some of those buildings don't look particularly safe to me.'

'I wasn't aware you're still on this case, Lieutenant.'

Shrugging, he went on, 'I guess that, officially, I'm not. Most of the evidence seems to have been passed to O'Leary. But I don't like loose ends hanging around. They're liable to trip you up when you aren't looking.'

I followed him into the nearest building. 'What do you reckon has happened to her?' I asked.

Without turning his head, he muttered, 'You want my opinion? I figure we're looking for a body here. My guess is that once Minton discovered she was seeing someone and then found out this guy's identity, he fingered them both to some pal of his in the Mobs. O'Leary was lucky to find Cortega's body so quickly. If that killing had been carried out properly he'd still be at the bottom of the Pacific. It would seem they took a little more trouble with the dame.'

He pushed open a door that was hanging on a single hinge. It fell inward with a crash that must have scared the rats half to death. Dust choked the back of my throat. There was nothing in the room and all of the glass had gone from the window.

'Nothing here,' he grunted in a disappointed tone. 'I reckon I'm just wasting my time. This is like searching for the proverbial needle in a haystack.'

He walked back towards the fallen door; then halted at a sudden shout from outside.

Going over to the large gap in the wall where the window had been I stared out. There was a cop standing on the opposite sidewalk. He was gesturing urgently with one hand. 'One of your men seems to have found something, Lieutenant,' I said.

Picking our way carefully over the litter and debris, we went outside and crossed over. 'What is it?' Morgan demanded.

The cop held out his right hand. Something glittered brilliantly in his palm. Morgan uttered a low whistle through his teeth. Picking it up he held it out towards me. It was a diamond and ruby earring and even at first glance I could see it was the real McCoy.

'Now that's something you don't usually find in a derelict dump like this,' I remarked. To the cop I said, 'Show us exactly where you found this.'

Morgan placed the earring inside a small plastic bag before following the guy into the warehouse. In was dark inside the building. Very little light came in through the gaps in the walls. Slabs of stone and bricks littered the dusty floor.

The cop took us to the far end of the large space before pointing towards one corner. Going down on one knee I examined the thick layer of dust. 'Did you go any further than this?' I asked.

He shook his head. 'It was lying just there.' He pointed towards a spot directly in front of me.

'Well, this dust has been disturbed but some attempt has been made to cover it up.' Glancing up at the Lieutenant, I went on, 'I reckon if you look carefully you'll find evidence of footprints although they'll be disturbed when this officer came in.'

'You're suggesting a body has been concealed here and then removed?' Morgan scratched his chin reflectively. 'That earring could have been pulled from her ear and left there unnoticed.'

'Perhaps. We've no absolute proof that it belonged to Barbara Minton although I'll admit it's stretching coincidence a bit too far to think it belonged to anyone else.'

We went back outside. Morgan looked pleased with what had happened. 'So I'm fairly certain her body was brought here. Then the killer probably figured there was a chance we'd start looking in places like this so he decided to move it.'

'That's a possibility,' I agreed.

He looked at me in surprise. 'You reckon there might be some other explanation?'

'From what you're saying, you seem convinced that Barbara Minton is dead. It's equally likely she's alive or at least she was when brought here. Maybe she took that earring out and left it to tell us something.'

He turned that over in his mind, watching his initial theory fall to pieces. Finally, he said grudgingly, 'I suppose that's possible. However, at the moment I'm keeping all my options open. In the meantime I'm taking this and checking if it did, indeed, belong to Barbara Minton. If so, it's the most significant clue we've got so far. Somehow, I doubt if we'll find her here, dead or alive.'

He was right, of course. But there was another thought in my mind as I made my way back to the car. The way I saw it, the killer had somehow known where Morgan intended to search and Barbara Minton had been removed from here in a hurry. It wasn't likely she'd come here of her own accord and then left again. However, most of these questions were about to be answered in the very near future.

I'd only just arrived at my office and settled myself in the chair when the door opened and O'Leary came in closely followed by Jack Kolowinski. As always there had been no polite knock. O'Leary just pushed his way in as though expecting to catch me in the middle of sniffing coke or some criminal act.

He sat down in the chair opposite me, leaving the Sergeant to stand just inside the door.

'You look as though you've got something important on your mind, Lieutenant,' I remarked.

'We've found Barbara Minton,' he said tightly, 'or at least, her body.'

'May I ask where you found her and how she was killed? I assume you came here to tell me this.'

'She was found in the basement of an empty block downtown. The janitor phoned the precinct less than an hour ago. The doctor and the forensic boys are examining the body right now. There doesn't seem to be much for them to look into. She was shot in the back of the head like Vinnie Cortega. I figured you ought to know to save you the trouble of going on with your search.'

'That was nice of you, Lieutenant. Tell me, when she was found was she wearing just one diamond and ruby earring?'

His eyebrows shot up so far they almost vanished under his hat. 'How the hell did you know that?'

'It's a long story, Lieutenant.'

'Long or not, you'll tell me now. If you're holding anything back, Merak, you'll find yourself in big trouble.'

'O.K. I've been out looking for her and bumped into Lieutenant Morgan. He — '

'Morgan!' O'Leary almost shouted the word. 'What's he doing on the case?'

'You'd better take that up with him,' I said evenly. 'Anyway he had some men with him down near the waterfront and one of the cops found this earring in one of the warehouses.'

'And where is it now?' O'Leary demanded.

'He's got it, of course.'

'I see.' O'Leary looked even less pleased than when he'd come in. 'I think I'll have to have a word with him.'

When he said nothing more, I asked, 'Anything else you want to tell me, Lieutenant?'

'Yes. Now that we've found Barbara

Minton I guess there's nothing more you need to do for her husband. I've got three murders on my hands and I don't need you poking your nose in.'

'I'll try to keep out of your way as much as possible,' I said sweetly.

'See that you do.' He got up. A moment later he left with Kolowinski trailing after him like a lost dog.

Twenty minutes later Dawn came in. As she sat down, she said, 'I hope your day was better than mine. I've been over most of downtown L.A. but nobody seems willing to talk. When I mentioned any protection they might be getting from some outfit they clam up completely. Don't want to talk about it. My guess is they're scared and from that I'd say this racket is still going on even after Cortega's death.'

'That doesn't surprise me,' I acknowledged. 'When you have a good scam going you try to keep it as long as possible.'

She nodded. 'Did you find out anything?'

'Quite a lot. I went out to the

waterfront where I met up with Morgan, the police lieutenant we met at the scene of the car fire. Like me, he was searching for Barbara Minton.'

'Did you find any sign of her?'

'One of the cops came across a valuable diamond earring in one of the warehouses. I don't think there's any doubt it was hers. Not that it matters now?'

Her eyes widened. 'Why do you say that?'

'O'Leary was in twenty minutes ago. They found Barbara's body a little while ago in the basement of some dump downtown. Shot in the head just like Cortega. Both sound to me like mob executions. There's a ritual killer somewhere out there, Dawn, and in spite of the fact that O'Leary has warned me off, I intend to find him, hopefully before there are any more murders.'

'You don't have much to go on,' she reminded me.

'I don't have anything to go on,' I told her. 'The only hope I have is that if I keep pushing hard enough this killer is going to make a mistake.'

136

'Just be careful you're not the one who slips up,' she said flatly.

I felt like a drink. There was some bourbon still left in the bottle in my drawer but I knew Dawn didn't approve of it during the afternoon so I settled for a coffee.

Ten minutes later as I was checking through the notes she had made during her visit downtown, the phone shrilled. I wasn't expecting anyone although those little mice inside my head were telling me that maybe Manzelli was beginning to get impatient and wanted to know how things were progressing.

However, it wasn't Manzelli. It was a voice I didn't recognize. 'Is that Johnny Merak, the private eye?' the voice asked. The guy sounded as though he wasn't quite sure he should be phoning me and might put the receiver down any minute.

'It is,' I said.

'I'd like to talk to you about these guys who're demanding dough from us. Some dame was round not long ago, said she worked for you and you were interested in what's going on around here.'

'Sure I'm interested,' I told him. 'But I don't like talking to people who don't give me their names.' The guy sounded funny as if he were looking over his shoulder all the time. It might have been a bad line but I didn't think so.

There was a long pause and I thought he'd put the phone down but a moment later, he said, 'I can't do that. I've got a wife and kids to think about and if they find out I've been talking my life won't be worth a bent dollar.'

'Do you know where my office is?'

'Sure I know. But I can't meet you there. It'll have to be somewhere where we can't be seen. Just you and me. Bring anyone with you and I won't be there.'

I felt those fingers of ice beginning to crawl along my spine. This had all the smell of a trap. It didn't sit right with me. Yet there was the possibility the speaker was the genuine article but scared to hell of the guys he was about to spill something on. I made up my mind at once.

'All right, friend. 'Do you know Mancini's bar?'

There was a further pause, then, 'Sure I know where it is. I'll meet you outside once it's dark. I don't want to be seen in daylight.' The line went dead.

Dawn had been watching me closely all the time I'd been speaking. As I put the receiver down, she asked quietly, 'Some unknown friend of yours, Johnny? It sounded to me as though you intend to meet him someplace. Do you think that's wise?'

Shrugging, I replied, 'I reckon he must know something. He mentioned that you'd been in the vicinity so I figure he's someone you spoke to.'

From the expression on her face I knew she still wasn't convinced it wasn't a trap but she said nothing more. It was dark when I stood on the sidewalk opposite Mancini's. There were few folk about. Mancini's looked its usual self. The dim light threw indistinct shadows across the dusty windows. I knew that Sergeant Kolowinski was a frequent visitor to the bar but I didn't want him butting in on this occasion. If my unknown friend even smelled the presence of anyone from the

LAPD around he'd vanish like smoke and my trip would have been completely wasted.

A couple of customers went inside as I stood there. I smoked a cigarette and then walked across the street, halting just to one side of the door. I didn't have to wait long before I spotted this fellow making his way along the sidewalk towards the bar. I knew from the way he kept looking over his shoulder that in all likelihood he was the man I was expecting. He studied me closely as he came forward, pausing a couple of feet away.

'Mister Merak?' he asked in a low whisper.

'That's right. You asked to meet me. What have you got on your mind.'

He came right up to me and clutched at my arm. 'Not here,' he hissed thinly. Turning swiftly on his heel, he hustled me into the narrow alley a couple of yards away. Not until he was satisfied the alley was deserted did he say in a low voice, 'You know about this crooked gangster Cortega?'

'He's dead.'

'So I've heard. But his outfit is still around and going strong. The guy who's taken over has only been boss for a couple of days but he's even worse than Cortega. His boys come around twice a week demanding money from all the shopkeepers in the district. Either we pay up or more of them come along and smash everything.'

'I suppose you've been to the cops.'

'Cops!' He uttered a low derisive laugh. 'What good would that do? Half of them get a backhander to look the other way. The others reckon there's no proof who's behind it.'

'So what do you want me to do about it?'

'I figured you might be able to help. They reckon you're in with the LAPD and the Feds. You seem to be interested in these hoodlums or that assistant of yours wouldn't be going around asking questions.'

'All right,' I said. 'I'm interested. But first I need to know the name of the boss who's now running this outfit.'

'O.K. I'll tell you. But you never heard

it from me. His name is — '

In that split second, a couple of shots rang out from somewhere near the far end of the alley. I reacted instinctively, dropping to my knees and pulling out the .38 in the same movement. The first slug had been intended for me. It struck the wall within an inch of my head as I went down. The second had been for my informant.

He'd been far too slow on the uptake. For a moment he stood in front of me and then fell sideways as the bullet hit him in the chest. Somewhere in the distance was the sound of running footsteps. I fired instinctively, heard the bullets ricochet off the wall in the distance. A few moments later there was the sound of a car roaring away into the darkness. It would be useless trying to follow the shooter. He'd be just another faceless killer carrying out orders from higher up. Bending, I lifted the dying man's head off the asphalt. Blood oozed from the side of his mouth and trickled slowly down his chin. His eyes were wide open, staring.

'Give me the name,' I hissed. Already there was a babble of voices coming from the nearby bar. Another couple of seconds and I'd have company. His lips twitched and for a moment I thought he wasn't going to make it. His voice was so low I could barely make out the single word. 'Santos'.

Then his whole body went limp. Glancing up I saw Mancini and Jack Kolowinski staring down at me. There were three other customers behind them.

'What the hell happened here, Johnny?' Kolowinski went down on one knee beside me.

'This guy met me here to give me some valuable information, Jack,' I told him, I pushed the .38 back into its holster. 'Somebody didn't want me to know it and decided to silence him permanently.'

'Where's this killer now?'

I jerked a thumb towards the end of the alley. 'He's miles away by now, Jack. There was a car waiting for him. But I'm sure I know who he's working for.'

Kolowinski scratched his chin, then swung on Mancini. 'Get back in there and phone Lieutenant O'Leary of the Homicide Squad,' he said tersely. As Mancini still hesitated, he snapped. 'Now!'

Mancini ran back into the bar. The small knot of early night customers remained, clustering around the dead guy.

Mancini must have got through to O'Leary right away and as was his usual style, the lieutenant didn't waste any time. The wail of a police siren sounded in the near distance less than ten minutes later, howling like a soul in Purgatory.

O'Leary pushed his way through the small group of onlookers. He saw me at once. 'Merak! I might have known. I thought I told you to stay out of this and keep your nose clean.'

'It's none of my doing, Lieutenant,' I told him. 'This guy phoned me and arranged to meet me here after dark. He said he didn't want to be seen. He — '

O'Leary held up a hand. 'I'll get your statement later,' he snapped. 'In the meantime I suggest you go into the bar and get yourself a drink.'

I did as I was told. Where O'Leary was concerned it was the best way. I could sometimes get around the Big Boys in the Organization but with O'Leary when he said you did something, you did it without any argument. Once inside the bar, I found a seat in my usual place and ordered a bourbon on the rocks. The guy behind the counter knew me and my drink was there within ten seconds.

I didn't have to wait too long before the door behind me swung open and the Lieutenant came in. His face was expressionless. Coming across to me he signalled towards one of the tables. Taking my drink with me, I sat down opposite him.

Pushing his hat onto the back of his head, he said tautly, 'All right, Merak, let's have it — from the beginning. You're mixed up in something and I want to know what it is. And I want none of this client confidentiality malarkey.'

I took a couple of sips of the bourbon before saying, 'There's not much to tell, Lieutenant. I got a phone call from that guy this afternoon. He wanted to talk to me but he was scared so we arranged this meeting place.'

'What exactly did he want to talk about?'

'I gathered it was about this protection racket that's started up someplace downtown. I sent Dawn Grahame there earlier today to ask around but nobody seemed inclined to talk.'

'But this guy was?'

'So he said. I know Vinnie Cortega was running the show but now he's dead I wanted to check whether someone else had taken over the outfit.'

O'Leary sat back and mulled that over in his mind for a couple of minutes before going on, 'So you met this guy and took him into the alley to pump him for information — is that the way of it?'

'For once, Lieutenant, you've got it right on the nose except he insisted on going there.'

'But someone else knew about this meeting and decided to take him out before he could spill anything.'

'I guess you're right a second time.'

'So how much did he tell you?'

'He just managed to give me a name before he snuffed it.'

O'Leary pressed his lips together into a hard thin line. Staring directly at me, he asked, 'And the name?'

'Santos.'

O'Leary repeated the name twice under his breath. I knew it didn't mean a thing to him but it went into that mental filing system he called a brain and I knew it would stay there until he'd found out everything there was to know about the guy.

'Is that all, Merak?' he asked finally.

'That's all.'

He gave me a hard look then pushed back his chair and got to his feet.

As he moved away I said thinly, 'Tell me, Lieutenant, do you intend to do anything about this protection racket? There's a guy out there who gave his life to get that information to me.'

O'Leary shrugged. 'This racket is nothing to do with homicide, Merak.'

'Maybe not. But there's a stiff out there and that sure as hell is.' I knew I'd hit a raw nerve.

Glaring at me, he hissed, 'Don't try to tell me how to do my job, Merak. You just stick to seeing old ladies across the street.' He hesitated, then went on stiffly, 'And for your information, I've just had one of your clients, Edward Minton, brought in on a charge of triple first-degree murder.'

I sat there and finished my drink. I had no idea what evidence O'Leary had for charging Minton with first-degree murder. Maybe the guy was getting desperate and knew he had to charge someone before the Commissioner began breathing down his neck and asking why he'd seen no results. Certainly there seemed to be quite a lot of circumstantial evidence against Barbara's husband but I doubted if any of it would stand up before a grand jury. However, I knew there was nothing I could say that would change his mind so I decided to let him go ahead and make a fool of himself — something he was quite capable of doing without my help.

Going over to the bar I ordered another drink. Twenty minutes later Kolowinski walked in without O'Leary. He got himself a drink and came over, lowering himself into the chair his boss had vacated earlier.

Over the rim of his glass, he said, 'I know how you feel, Johnny. But O'Leary's a good cop. He's just doing his job.'

'Sure. And I'm trying to do mine but he's not making it any easier. And what the hell prompted him to arrest Minton? He must know he can't possibly make a case against him.'

'He thinks he can so he's going ahead with it.'

'Then I wish him luck. He's going to need it.'

★   ★   ★

When I left Mancini's there was no sign of the body. I guessed the doctor and the forensic boys had been, seen all they needed to see, and the body had been taken along to the morgue. I didn't know his name. He was just some guy who'd wanted to do something to help his neighbours and had paid for it.

There was still a heat in the air as I

walked back to my car and climbed in behind the wheel. I'd left Kolowinski seated morosely at the table staring down at his drink. Sooner or later he'd get up and go home. Normally it would be much later, sometime during the early hours of the morning. How much longer it could go on before his superiors found out about his drinking habits, I didn't know. But I had the feeling that his pension was rapidly disappearing into the sunset. That was a pity because I rather liked the guy.

I got back to my apartment twenty minutes later, made myself a drink, and decided to have an early night. This case was beginning to get to me. There were so many things happening one on top of the other and very few of them made any sense. I was sure of one thing however. Minton wasn't involved in his wife's murder or any other. Those little mice were telling me he had the best motive in the world — money. That, I thought, was the reason O'Leary intended to pull him in. But I had the gut feeling there was someone else out there, someone who was planning and executing these seemingly random murders and the trouble was I couldn't put my finger on him. Yet in spite of that, these gut feelings had served me well in the past.

I finished my drink, thought of pouring out another one but then decided against it. Sleep was what I needed to keep a clear head. The one thought in my mind before I fell asleep was: Just why had Manzelli started all of this when he had tossed that newspaper onto my desk. What did he know that I didn't?

★   ★   ★

The next morning I was dragged from a dreamless sleep by the shrilling of the phone in the next room. A quick glance at my watch told me it was only a little after eight. Stumbling out of the bed I made it to the table and sank down into the chair. Picking up the receiver, wondering who might be calling at this early hour, I said hoarsely, 'Merak?'

A woman's voice that sounded vaguely familiar said, 'I'm glad I managed to reach you before you left for your office, Mister Merak. I have to talk to you urgently.'

Furrowing my brows, I asked, 'Who is this?' Her voice sounded like that of a woman who expected her every order to be carried out immediately and with no questions.

'Ophelia Silworth.'

The name cleared my brain at once. I couldn't imagine why she wanted to speak to me but I guessed I'd soon find out.

'There is something important I must discuss with you as soon as possible. When can you see me?'

'I'll be in my office within half an hour if that's convenient,' I said.

There was a pause while she seemed to be considering that. Finally, she made up her mind. 'Very well. I'll be there.'

Putting down the receiver, I sat back and lit a cigarette. The bottle of bourbon was still on the table beside me together with an empty glass. I considered it for a moment but then decided against it. My head was pounding like a jackhammer and I knew that would only make it worse. After swallowing a couple of aspirins I got dressed, made a couple of sandwiches, then set off for the office.

No one was there when I arrived. I knew it would be another half hour before Dawn showed up. I opened the window. Already the air inside the room was stifling.

I didn't have to wait long however. I had just unlocked the filing cabinet when the door opened and Ophelia Silworth entered. She looked around her as if wondering why she had agreed to come to a place like this. Motioning her to the chair, I said, 'How can I help you, Mrs, Silworth?'

She came to the point straight away. 'You know, of course, that my daughter has been murdered?'

'Yes,' I nodded. 'And apparently in the same manner as the man she was seeing.'

'I want you to find out who did it.'

'You realize, of course, that this is purely a police matter? Wouldn't it be better to leave it in their hands. Lieutenant O'Leary of the homicide division doesn't take too kindly to private detectives muscling in on his cases.'

She gave a frosty smile at that last remark. 'Personally I don't consider this Lieutenant O'Leary to be very good at his job. I'd much prefer someone like yourself who isn't averse to bending the law a little when it suits you.'

I tried to look hurt. 'I hope you're not suggesting that I deliberately break the law.'

'Believe me, I know more about you than you realize. If I pay anyone to undertake work for me, I first find out everything about them. You were once a part of the Mafia here in Los Angeles. I think you know more about them than any member of the police.'

I considered that. What she said was undoubtedly true but I didn't want it spread around — it might have the effect of frightening off potential customers in the future.

'Very well, I'll look into your daughter's murder but I'm not promising anything. Furthermore, if you've no objections, there are a few questions I'd like to ask you while you're here.'

I couldn't analyze the expression on her face but I had the impression she hadn't expected that and didn't know how to react.

At last, however, she nodded. 'What is it you want to know?'

'Firstly, according to the report in the newspaper, your daughter was coming back from visiting you when she vanished. Apparently her father was ill. Is that true?'

She hesitated and then shook her head. 'I don't know where the papers got that information but my husband is perfectly well, has been for several years.'

'I see. I'm now going to ask you a very personal question so please don't take offence. How well did you and your husband get on with your daughter? Was there any animosity between you?'

Her head went up at that and her face hardened like granite. 'I hope you're not suggesting that either my husband or myself had anything to do with what happened to her!' She spat the words at me like individual sparks. For a moment I thought she meant to lean forward over the desk and slap me across the face. With an effort, she controlled herself.

'Not at all,' I assured her hastily.

'I'm glad of that.' Calming down a little, she went on, 'Naturally neither of us was pleased when we discovered she was playing around with this man Cortega. We did our best to put an end to it, even offering him a large sum of money.'

'But he didn't accept your offer?'

'No.' There was bitterness in her tone now. 'He tried to persuade us that he was really in love with her and wanted her to leave Edward. It was all an act, of course. I could see right through him.'

I'll bet you could, I thought. And you'd be right. No doubt he was looking to the future when it might be possible for him to get his hands on all of her dough.

'Well, you've been very open with me, Mrs. Silworth. I'll certainly do my best to find her killer. I would suggest you don't mention my involvement to the police.'

'I understand.' She rummaged inside her bag and took out an envelope that she slid across the desk towards me as she rose elegantly to her feet. 'I take it I'll be hearing from you in due course.'

'As soon as I find out anything you'll be the first to know,' I told her.

Letting her out, I closed the door and went back to my chair. There was five thousand dollars inside the envelope. Not as much as Edward Minton had given me but I guess that even those who own a diamond empire are careful with their money. Or perhaps she thought that was all I was worth.

Dawn came in a little while later and while we drank our morning coffee, I told her all that had happened. She looked serious by the time I'd finished. 'Don't you think you're taking on a lot, Johnny? Very soon you're going to have Manzelli breathing down your neck and I reckon he can be more dangerous than Ophelia Silworth.'

She was right, of course. No one made a mistake where Manzelli was concerned. Otherwise it was likely to be the last one you ever made. The Big Boss had said that the death threats he'd received had originated with the arrival in L.A. of

157

Cortega. What I wanted to know was — now that Cortega was dead, had the threats stopped? If they had it seemed likely he'd been behind them. That would be my job finished. But if not, then there was still some shadowy figure out there that I knew nothing about. I didn't like that thought but it was something to consider.

The big question was how to get that information. No one got directly in touch with Manzelli. The only way was to ring one of his henchmen and put the question through him. That was what I decided to do.

I dialled his number and waited. The phone rang for more than a minute before anyone answered. Then some guy came on.

Swallowing hard, I said, 'This is Johnny Merak. Mister Manzelli asked me to find out some information for him.'

'So?' grated the voice. 'Do you have any?'

'My understanding is that your boss has received certain threats against him which he had cause to believe were genuine. Since they coincided with the arrival in L.A. of a certain hoodlum named Vinnie Cortega he suspected these threats came from him. Now that Cortega is dead, can you tell me if these threats have stopped?'

After a momentary hesitation, the guy said, 'I'll make inquiries. Someone will contact you.'

'Will it be Manzelli himself?' I didn't know why I asked that question. It just came out of my mouth without warning.

'That will depend entirely upon Mister Manzelli.' The line went dead with a click that sounded like the crack of doom.

As I lit a cigarette and blew the smoke towards the ceiling I thought: Well at least Manzelli knows I'm still working on the case. How much more he knew about the Barbara Minton affair I didn't know.

Dawn and I spent the rest of the day going over everything we knew trying to make sense out of everything. There was very little we had to go on but shortly before we closed for the night the telephone rang. I'd expected that when Manzelli eventually got in touch with me it would be one of his underlings on the line. This time, however, it wasn't. It was the Godfather himself.

'Mister Merak,' he said in that soft, but menacing, tone. 'I understand you've been inquiring about these death threats I've been receiving.'

'That's correct.' I said.

'It would appear that my initial surmise as to the identity of the sender was wrong. I appreciate that this man Cortega is dead and you were working on the hypothesis that he was the one responsible.'

'That's also correct,' I told him. Those little mice, scurrying around inside my head, were telling me I was about to be told something I didn't particularly want to hear. Manzelli's next words confirmed that they were right.

'Unfortunately I received another this afternoon.'

'Was it exactly the same as the others?'

'It was — in every detail. I'm afraid you're going to have to look further. And I'm sure I don't have to remind you that I require results as soon as possible. I have no wish to depart this life any sooner than I must. Can I look forward to hearing from you again within the next few days? This time I shall want a name and proof. Once I receive that you may leave everything else to me.'

'I'll do everything I possibly can,' I told him. 'But whoever this guy is he's covered his tracks well.'

'Do you have any idea at all who he is?'

'I may be way off the track,' I replied, 'but I have the feeling he's the same person who's committed all of these other murders.'

'Oh?' Manzelli feigned surprise. 'Why do you say that? Do you have any proof to link me with any of those who've been murdered?'

'Nothing definite. But my hunches have usually been right and — '

'Mister Merak. I did not hire you to act on hunches.' His tone was softer now and for some reason that made it more sinister. 'You haven't failed me in the past. I sincerely hope you don't now.'

The threat behind his words was so obvious it sizzled down the line. There was a short pause and then the phone went dead.

Reaching for her coat, Dawn said, 'I gather that was Manzelli on the phone.'

'It was,' I told her. 'And he wasn't very pleased. More than that he sounded real scared and that's something I've never known before. I don't like it. When guys like Manzelli are frightened they're liable to do anything and if he decides I'm not doing things right and quickly enough, it's possible there might be one less Johnny Merak in the world.'

★　★　★

The following morning I got word from O'Leary that Edward Minton had been arrested for his wife's murder, together with that of Vinnie Cortega. There was no mention of Jim Baker but I guessed O'Leary was holding that one back just in case he couldn't make a case against the other two.

Before he got off the phone, I asked, 'Is it possible for me to see Minton. After all he is my client and as far as I know he hasn't hired any other lawyer.'

'I'll ask him whether he wants to see you, Merak. Since the only law training you've had is getting yourself out of trouble with the police and the Mobs, I doubt it. I reckon he'll need the best lawyer he can get.'

I had to wait another hour before the Lieutenant got back to me. He sounded disappointed as he said, 'Minton will see you, Merak. I'm holding him here if you care to come down to the precinct.'

'I'll be there in twenty minutes,' I told him.

I decided to take Dawn with me. It wasn't just that she was pretty good at spotting anything that didn't add up — she also added a touch of class to the proceedings.

At the precinct we were shown into a small cell. Minton was seated behind the desk looking sorry for himself. We went in. A plain-clothed cop stood just inside the door. I eyed him up and down before saying, 'I don't need you in the room.'

'I'm here on Lieutenant O'Leary's orders,' the other said stiffly.

163

'I don't give a damn who gave the orders. This man in my client and whatever is said during our conversation is strictly private and confidential. If you've got a problem with that send in O'Leary.'

He didn't like that but he turned and went out of the room. Through the window I saw him talking animatedly with the Lieutenant. After a couple of minutes the cop went back to a desk on the far side of the room. O'Leary paused for a moment and then went back to his own desk. Obviously he didn't intend to push his point too far.

'All right, Mister Minton,' I said, 'let's get down to hard facts. Did you kill Cortega and your wife?'

'I'd nothing to do with it,' he declared. 'How could I have killed them? I didn't know about Cortega or where my wife was.'

'That won't be enough to convince a grand jury. There's plenty of evidence to suggest you knew about this affair and who your wife's lover was before either of them were shot. The police reckon they were both killed some time on the same day as Cortega's body was discovered washed up on the beach. Where were you that day?'

'I was at home. Some of the servants must have seen me.'

Beside me, Dawn was jotting down what Minton said in her notebook. Looking up, she said, 'But you wouldn't be in sight of the servants all of the time. There would be times during the day when you could easily have slipped out and shot Cortega.'

'And take his body out to sea and drop it overboard from one of those three yachts I understand you own,' I added. 'I figure the only way we can clear you is to find out who the real killer is.'

'Did you ever mention Cortega to any of your friends or acquaintances?' Dawn inquired.

'I can't remember. I was angry at the time and I'd also had something to drink. It's possible I suppose but I don't think so.' He shifted uncomfortably in his chair. 'If I did mention him to anyone I guess it would have been Lieutenant Morgan. He asked me a lot of questions at the time we found her burnt-out car.'

'I can't imagine him killing the two of them even if he was paid to do so,' I remarked. 'When we found them it seemed obvious to me they were both execution-style murders. Something the Organization would carry out, not a copper.'

'So it could be virtually anyone?' There was now a hopeless note in Minton's voice. He sat with his head in his hands staring straight ahead of him.

Just as that moment the door behind me opened and this guy came in. From the dapper suit and the briefcase he carried I guessed he was Minton's attorney. I reckoned he was somewhere in his mid-fifties. Seating himself in the chair at the end of the desk, he threw Dawn and I an inquiring glance. The expression on his face suggested that he hadn't expected to find anyone else with his client and he was wondering what the hell we were doing there.

'This is Carl Winters, my lawyer,' Minton said. 'These are Johnny Merak and his assistant, Dawn Grahame.'

Winters made no attempt to shake hands and his frosty expression didn't change. 'Are you lawyers too?' he asked thinly.

Before I could say anything, Minton said, 'Mister Merak is a private investigator. I hired him some time ago when Barbara disappeared.'

'So why is he here now?' Winters asked sharply.

'I'm hoping he'll be able to find the real killer.'

Winters snapped open his briefcase and took out some papers that he placed on the desk in front of him with an exaggerated care. Then he stared directly at me. 'To be quite honest, Mister Merak, I can see no reason why you should still be on this case. We know what happened to Barbara. Once I put all of the facts in front of a grand jury I'm certain they'll find we haven't a case to answer.'

'I wouldn't be too sure of that,' I said. 'I've had dealings with the cops for a long time, especially Lieutenant O'Leary. He wouldn't have arrested our friend here unless he could prove motive, means and opportunity. From what Mister Minton has told me, he had all three, enough to satisfy the D.A.'

Winters didn't look too pleased at that. Twisting his lips into a scowl, he said, 'I suggest you leave the law to me, Mister Merak. Just stick to your detective work.'

Shrugging, I pushed back my chair and got up. 'Very well. I'll do that.' I glanced across the table at Minton. 'At the moment, you're still my client. It's entirely up to you if you want me to continue looking into this case.'

He bit his lower lip. Evidently, with Winters sitting there, he wasn't sure what to do for the best. Finally he nodded. 'Just see what you can find out.'

'I will,' I said as I opened the door for Dawn. Just as I stepped outside, I heard Winters say, 'I believe you're a fool paying a private detective. It's my job to represent you in court.'

Closing the door, I said to Dawn, 'You know Dawn, I get the feeling that this attorney reckons that Minton is guilty but just so long as he gets paid he couldn't care less.'

'Why do you say that, Johnny?'

'I suppose it's the way he was so quick to dismiss the possibility there might be someone else responsible.'

'So you're sure he's innocent?'

'I'm damned sure he is. Everything fits together too perfectly for my liking. It's all too easy.'

Besides, I told myself, I had this hunch that our killer was the same person who had shot the private detective, Baker and also sent those threatening notes to Manzelli. In spite of the fact that logically it didn't make all that much sense, the notion wouldn't go away.

5

The Killer Strikes Again

The next day dawned just like any other day. The sun came up and the temperature began to rise quickly. It was going to be another scorcher where most folk walked in the shade and the air conditioning units were turned up to maximum.

Despite the fact that everything seemed normal enough on the surface I woke with the gut feeling that something unexpected was about to happen. Even after eating the excellent breakfast that Dawn prepared, this notion refused to go away. The first indication that I might be right came fifteen minutes after I got into the office.

The phone rang. It was O'Leary on the line. He sounded as if the entire world and its worries had just landed on his shoulders. 'I thought I'd let you know that Edward Minton had just been released,' he said. 'Someone posted a million dollar bail for him.'

'How the hell did he manage that?' I asked.

'It seems that attorney of his has pulled some strings and found some judge willing to grant it. We opposed bail, of course, since he's wanted for first-degree murder and it was strongly opposed by Mrs. Silworth. But there was nothing we could do.'

'And has a date been fixed for his trial?'

'Yeah. Six weeks from today.'

'I see.' I didn't really. It was highly unusual for bail to be granted in these circumstances. As the Lieutenant had said, there was someone behind the scenes pulling the strings — but why? Who would want him out of jail and be willing to put up such a high bail? I knew of only one man who had sufficient dough and enough pull to sway a judge and that was Manzelli.

Certainly Minton had some connection with the Godfather. He'd admitted as much when I'd first met him. How close the two were was something I didn't know and my guess was that Minton would never tell me.

There was, however, someone who might know and someone who might be ready to spill everything she knew, especially if it might get Minton back behind bars until the trial — his mother-in-law, Ophelia Silworth!

I didn't know her telephone number but Dawn was pretty quick in getting hold of the directory for Colorado and finding it for me. I rang the number, waited for a few moments, and then she came on the line.

'Hello. Who is this?' she inquired.

'Johnny Merak,' I replied. 'You may remember you came to see me a little while ago.'

There was a pause and then, 'Oh yes, I remember. The private investigator.'

'The same. I believe you know that your son-in-law has been released on bail.'

'So I've heard.' There was no inflection in her voice but I could sense the anger in it. It flowed like vitriol along the line and into my ear. 'Do you know who put up all that money and persuaded the judge to grant bail?'

'I'm afraid not. But you may be able to help me there.'

'In what way? I'm just as much in the dark as you are.'

I tried to put my questions as discreetly as possible. Ophelia Silworth was the kind of woman who'd either go along with you all the way, or shut up like a clam.

'I know that your son-in-law has some connections with the gangs in Los Angeles. The problem is that I'm not sure how deeply involved he is with them. It may be he simply puts certain contracts in their way. That happens all the time. On the other hand, it may be something more serious. I was wondering whether you've heard anything.'

There was a long silence from which I knew she was aware of something but unsure whether to pass it on to someone like me. To coax her into spilling it all, I added, 'I can promise you that whatever you tell me won't go any further than this office.'

Finally, she reached a decision. 'Very

well. I'll tell you what I know. I suspected he was into dealing in armaments some years ago, bringing weapons into this country for certain gangsters in a number of cities, not just Los Angeles. He was married to Barbara at that time so I decided to keep my mouth shut. But I kept on probing. If it had been illegal drugs I would have reported it to the police at once.'

'But if a few of the mobs gun themselves down it would be fewer on the streets?'

'I suppose you could put it that way.' The acid in her tone was even more pronounced now.

'Did you find out which of the outfits he was working with?' I knew it was a long shot but there was the possibility she did know something.

'Edward did mention a name once but I took little notice of it at the time. It was a foreign name. Italian, I think.'

'Was it Rizzio?'

A pause and then, 'No, I'm sure that wasn't it. Mantella — no, Manzelli. That was the name.'

That was something I didn't want to hear. If it had been Sam Rizzio I might have been able to find out more. But no one with more sense than a crayfish would think of poking into Manzelli's business. Do that and you stood less chance of living than diving head first off a thousand-foot cliff.

'You've been extremely helpful, Mrs. Silworth,' I said. 'In the meantime, I'll keep a close eye on Edward Minton. If he breaks the term of his bail I'll be sure to let Lieutenant O'Leary know.' I put the phone down. Things were beginning to hot up but I still didn't like the way they were going.

But there was one little thought in my mind. Was it possible that for some reason Minton had got on the wrong side of Manzelli and had to be eliminated? It wouldn't be easy for him to get to Minton while he was in jail. But if he was out on bail, the chances of him being killed increased a thousand-fold.

I voiced my suspicions to Dawn. Quite often in the past what she called her feminine intuition enabled her to spot any flaws in my reasoning. She waited until I'd finished; then chewed it over in her mind for a little while.

Finally, she said seriously, 'From what she says it would seem that Manzelli is the logical candidate for these murders. That doesn't make it easy for you, does it?'

'It doesn't. I — '

The phone rang again interrupting my flow of thoughts. As I picked it up I hoped it wasn't either O'Leary or Manzelli. It wasn't. Edward Minton's voice said, 'Is that you, Merak?'

'The same. I gather you're a free man now until the trial. I don't know how you pulled that off but — '

'That's what I need to talk to you about — urgently.'

This wasn't what I'd expected but he was still my client so I decided to go along with him. 'I can't see why you should want to talk to me,' I began.

'Are you free this evening? I wouldn't suggest this but in view of what's happened I must see you. Can you come to my place about nine?'

I considered his request. I might get myself in big trouble if anyone found out I was seeing him while he was on bail. Then I thought — what the hell? I was perfectly within my rights to consult with my client at any time. 'I'll be there,' I said.

* * *

My watch said five minutes before nine as I parked in front of the Minton mansion on the outskirts of L.A. It was a big place, set in its own grounds, with a long gravel drive leading up to it from the road. There were lights in the lower windows.

Going up to the door I rang the bell. It was answered a couple of minutes later by a guy in a black monkey suit who eyed me suspiciously. He was possibly wondering why I hadn't gone round to the rear entrance instead of showing up there.

'I've an appointment with Mister Edward Minton,' I said.

His expression didn't change. However, he'd obviously been told I was expected and stood on one side to let me in. It was growing dark outside and the bright lights hurt my eyes for a moment.

'You'll be Mister Merak, I presume,' the flunkey said. He still had that supercilious tone that grated on my nerves.

'You've guessed right.'

'If you'll follow me I'll take you to Mister Minton.'

He led the way along a wide corridor, expensively decorated. Whether the paintings on the walls had been for the benefit of his late wife, or were his own taste in art, I didn't know. Me — I wouldn't have given them houseroom.

Opening a door on the left, he ushered me inside. The room was big. You could have held a banquet for fifty people in it with room to spare around the edges. Minton was standing by the large window. He turned as I went in. His expression was more serious than I'd ever seen it.

'Thank you for coming, Merak,' he said soberly. 'Please sit down.'

I lowered myself gingerly into a delicately-carved chair that looked as if a miracle were required for it to bear my weight. He remained standing and there was something in his attitude that gave me the feeling he was ready to run at any second.

'I gather you've something important on your mind.' I said.

Before replying, he went to the cabinet at one side of the room. Lifting the whiskey decanter he poured out two glasses and brought them over. Placing one in front of me, he said tightly, 'I've been trying to figure out who got me out on bail — and why.'

'Don't you know who it was?' I asked, surprised.

He shook his head. 'I've no idea. But I must confess that worries me a lot.'

Watching his face closely, I asked, 'Do you think it was Manzelli?'

He looked genuinely surprised, then shook his head. 'I know of no reason why Manzelli would do that. We weren't all that close.'

'So what are you worried about?'

He remained silent for a full minute, biting his lower lip. There was something on his mind but he seemed to have trouble getting it out. Then the words came out in a rush. 'I'm sure someone is out to kill me. Once I was arrested and locked up they missed their chance. Somehow they had to get me out in the open again and this is how they did it.'

I'd considered that possibility earlier and now he was confirming it. I drank down some of the whiskey. I noticed he hadn't touched his. He remained on his feet, walking up and down the room, as if unable to sit still.

'Then why are you still here? If it's not a condition of your bail that you have to remain here, I'd get away to somewhere in the country and stay out of sight until the trial.'

His lips twisted into what was more of a grimace than a smile. 'I'm figuring on doing just that,' he said harshly. 'But first I wanted this talk with you. Just in case anything happens to me I want you to know that I'm not intending to skip bail. You'll be able to tell — '

There was a small sound like glass shattering. For a brief moment he remained standing there as if nothing had happened. Then he sagged awkwardly as his knees bent and he went forward onto his face on the thick carpet. The glass fell from his fingers, the drink spilling over the rich pile. From the way he'd gone down, I knew he was dead before he hit the floor.

Running to the window, I stared out into the darkness. There was a quick movement in the distance. I glimpsed the killer among the bushes about thirty yards away, just an indistinct, anonymous shape that disappeared within seconds. Nearer at hand there was a neat, circular hole in the glass and shards of it on the floor.

Going back to the body, I noticed the spreading red stain on his white shirt. Whoever had fired that shot was an excellent marksman. The slug had taken Minton right through the heart.

A moment later the door opened and the manservant came in. His wide-eyed gaze passed from the body on the floor to me. His mouth opened but nothing came out.

'Get on to the police and ask for Lieutenant O'Leary,' I said thinly. 'Tell him what's happened. I doubt if it'll help for them to throw a cordon around this place. That killer will be miles away before they get here.'

The guy just stood there as if carved from granite, staring down at the body.

'Don't just stand there like a bloody fool. Did you hear what I said? Get on the phone and ask for Lieutenant O'Leary.' I raised my voice. Somehow I got through to him. I gave him the Lieutenant's number.

Turning on his heel he hurried towards the phone on the desk. He spoke hurriedly for a couple of minutes and then put the phone down. Coming over to where I knelt by the body, he quavered, 'What happened, sir?'

Without looking up, I snapped, 'Someone shot him from outside in the grounds. From what he told me he had an idea that somebody was out to get him. It seems he was right.'

'But who would want to shoot the master?' My companion was having trouble taking everything in.

'If I knew that I'd have something to

tell the cops when they get here.'

I knew there'd be very little traffic around at that time of the evening and wasn't surprised when two police cars drove up to the house fifteen minutes later with their sirens wailing like lost souls in Purgatory. O'Leary was there looking as angry as ever, closely followed by Kolowinski.

I got to my feet as he entered the room. 'This is getting to be a habit, Merak,' he snarled. 'A bad habit. I won't ask what you're doing here. Once I get a call that someone had been rubbed out I know you'll be close by. However, you can start by answering a few questions.'

'You know I always try to be of help, Lieutenant,' I said.

He gave me a funny look but that was all. Tilting his hat onto the back of his head, he went on, 'What were you doing here at this time of night?'

'Minton asked me to come. He said there was something he wanted to talk about.'

'And do you know what it was?'

'He was under the impression that

someone was out to kill him.'

O'Leary sniffed. 'He wasn't far out on that. Did you see who fired the shot? There's an excellent view from this window.' He pointed. 'From the trajectory of the slug I'd say the killer was somewhere close to those bushes.'

'Sure. I caught a brief glimpse of someone running back towards the road yonder but it was too dark to make out much.'

'Could you say whether it was a man or woman?' Kolowinski spoke up for the first time.

'I wouldn't like to swear to either, Sergeant,' I replied. 'Everything was happening so fast. All I saw was an indistinct shape making off across the grass.'

O'Leary went down on one knee beside the body, his face twisted into a mask of concentration. Finally, he muttered, 'I'd say our killer used a rifle for this job. It's all of thirty yards to those bushes and there's no cover closer to this window.'

'I'd go along with that,' I agreed. 'And whoever it was he was a damned good shot. I know Minton would make an excellent target silhouetted against the light in here. But I'd say that bullet got him right through the heart.'

O'Leary turned his attention to the manservant. 'Have there been any visitors here today?'

'No, sir. After the master was released on bail there's been no one calling here. I was informed that Mister Merak would be coming at nine o'clock but as far as I'm aware no one else was expected.'

'Do you have any idea who might want to kill him?' O'Leary swung his gaze in my direction. 'You seem to know more than anyone else.'

'I'd say the person who killed him is the one who arranged to get him released on bail. But whether we're dealing with two killers or just one, I don't know.'

'How do you figure it was the same person who had him released?'

'Isn't it obvious? Someone wanted him dead but getting to him would be somewhat difficult while he was in custody. They had to get him out of jail first. Once that was accomplished it would be relatively easy to pick him off whenever the opportunity presented itself.'

'That makes sense, I suppose,' he admitted grudgingly.

'It's the only logical explanation.'

He rubbed his chin. It was like running the edge of a knife along sandpaper. 'Then it should reduce the number of possible suspects. We're obviously looking for someone with that kind of dough and have enough clout to swing the judge.' There was an expression on his face I didn't like.

'I know what you're thinking, Lieutenant. You reckon our man is Enrico Manzelli. I'm sorry, but I don't buy that.'

'Can you think of anyone else who fits the bill?' There was a note of triumph in his tone.

'Not at the moment. But, somehow, I'm sure you're wrong about Manzelli.'

O'Leary drew his lips back across his teeth. 'Why? Because he's some kind of friend of yours?'

I knew he was trying to rile me, get me to say something I didn't want to say.

Trying to keep my temper, I said, 'If you think you can bring Manzelli in on a charge of multiple murder, go ahead. But my guess is you won't find a judge in L.A. willing to sign a warrant.'

'We'll see about that. No one, not even Manzelli, is above the law.'

'Then I wish you luck. Now if you've no further questions, I'd like to go.'

He gave me an ugly look. 'I've no doubt I'll think of a lot more. In the meantime you can go.'

I passed another couple of guys on the way out. I'd no doubt they were the forensic people. Not that there would be much for them to find. One dead body and a bullet hole in the window. If O'Leary went ahead with his plan to bring in the Big Boss I didn't envy his job.

I decided to go back to Dawn's place. I needed to talk to someone who was willing to listen. She'd given me a key to her apartment some time before and I let myself in. She was sitting on the couch when I went in. Giving me a quick, inquiring glance she got to her feet and kissed me before getting me a drink and pouring one for herself.

'Something has happened,' she said quietly, 'I can see it written all over your face.'

'I went along to see Edward Minton. Apparently he had something important on his mind.'

Looking at me intently over the rim of her glass, she asked, 'Did he tell you what it was?'

'He had the idea someone was out to kill him.'

'And — ?'

'It seems he couldn't have been more right. Someone shot him from the grounds outside the window.'

'Then he's dead.' She said it quietly and calmly, almost as if she had been expecting it.

'As the proverbial dodo. Shot down right in front of me. O'Leary is there now with Jack Kolowinski. I'm afraid that very soon there's going to be big trouble.'

'Oh? In what way?'

'He suspects that Manzelli is the killer — or at least one of his boys acting on his orders. At the moment he's talking about arresting him on a murder charge.'

'I can see the problem, Johnny. If he does that it's likely to start a gang war against the police. Isn't there anything you can do?'

'Me? O.K. I'm absolutely sure Manzelli isn't involved in these killings unless he's lying about getting these threatening notes. The only way I can get O'Leary to see sense is to find out who the real killer is — and that's about as easy as breaking into Fort Knox.'

'Do you think you should let Manzelli know what O'Leary is planning?'

I pondered that for a little while; then decided against it. If Manzelli didn't know already, he soon would.

The following day I went through the local newspaper searching for any indication that O'Leary had carried out his threat. There was nothing. Had Manzelli been arrested for Minton's murder it would have been splashed right across the front page. My guess was that the lieutenant had had second thoughts. After all, there was no real evidence to link Manzelli with Minton. Their previous association would have been kept safely under wraps.

I wondered whether Ophelia Silworth was aware that her son-in-law had been murdered. It would be in all of the early editions in L.A. but whether she received copies in Colorado I didn't know.

I gave it to Dawn to check that I hadn't missed anything. 'Nothing here.' she said finally.

I had the feeling we were overlooking something important. Five people murdered and there had to be a common denominator linking them all together. My first suspect had been Edward Minton. I could imagine how his wife's infidelity would affect his social position as well as the natural anger at finding she was cheating on him. That would be a strong motive for killing his unfaithful wife and her lover.

He could also have killed James Baker if he suspected that the private investigator might discover something about his own past that he wanted to remain hidden. I wasn't sure about the guy who'd been shot in the alley before he could spill everything about the protection racket. Now, however, that theory had been blown out of the window. There was no doubt I'd been on the wrong track.

There was someone else; someone who was not only clever and cunning, but was keeping one step of me all the way.

The phone rang shrilly. Picking it up, I said, 'Merak.'

A voice I didn't recognize said harshly, 'There's a car waiting outside, Merak. Please don't keep the driver waiting.'

I knew at once who had sent the car. In a way I was surprised Manzelli hadn't been in touch before. He was not a man noted for his patience.

Getting up, I replaced the phone and said, 'Manzelli wants to see me, Dawn. I guess he's not very pleased he hasn't heard from me.'

Dawn had the same worried expression on her face whenever the Big Boss' name was mentioned. I knew what she was thinking. One of these days Manzelli would send for me and I wouldn't come back.

'Don't worry your pretty head. I'll be back in time for lunch.'

'I hope so.'

I went outside The big black limousine was waiting with one guy standing with the rear door open and the other sitting behind the wheel. I got in.

Twenty minutes later I was sitting in Manzelli's office facing him across the large desk. His expression told me nothing. But that wasn't surprising. No one knew what Manzelli was thinking. You only found that out when you were either leaving in one piece or you departed this world, hopefully for a better one.

'I'm quite sure you know why you're here, Mister Merak,' he began in that soft, menacing voice. 'If my memory serves me well, I recall that I did warn you against getting involved with Barbara Minton. My only reason for visiting you that morning was to hire you to find out who is threatening me. Why didn't you heed my warning of the danger associated with that case?'

I knew I had to choose my words very

carefully now if I wanted to get out of this meeting alive. Very slowly, I said, 'I suppose it's the detective in me. You made it sound sufficiently intriguing to excite my curiosity.'

'Ah, yes, your natural curiosity. And no doubt you believe that my words were intended to ensure that you did decide to investigate the case, even if it meant pushing my case into the background.'

This is where it's going to get tricky, I thought. One word that Manzelli didn't like and I was finished. That was as certain as the sun coming up the next day.

'That isn't quite the case,' I said finally, clearing my throat. 'You see, almost from the beginning I had the feeling that both cases were linked. I soon discovered that this hoodlum Cortega was not only seeing Minton's wife but was also head of this racket in downtown L.A. My guess was that he was the one who sent you those threats and the more I found out about him, the better. It's also the reason I needed to know if you'd received further threats after he'd been found shot.'

'I see.' He placed the tips of his fingers together. He seemed to be trying to decide whether I was lying or not. Leaning forward as far as his size would allow, he suddenly switched the subject. 'I have heard rumours that certain members of the Homicide Squad in the L.A.P.D. are of the opinion that I am the person behind these killings. May I ask what you think of that?'

'I think that Lieutenant O'Leary is way off the mark there,' I replied quickly, forcing conviction into my voice.

'I'm pleased to hear that.' He sat back. 'Do you have any ideas about who the real killer is?'

'Not at the moment,' I admitted. 'With Minton dead, my only lead has gone.'

'A pity you didn't question him before he was released from custody. But I'm confident you'll soon discover the identity of the killer. I hope my confidence isn't misplaced.'

I waited for him to say something more but instead he merely waved a hand to indicate the meeting was over. I could feel the sweat dripping into my eyes as I left.

The limousine was waiting together with the same two guys. The journey back to my office was the mirror image of my outward trip. Both of my companions remained as silent as the grave during the entire journey.

Dawn looked as surprised as I felt that I was still walking around on my two feet. 'Would you like a coffee?' she asked.

'I could certainly use one,' I replied.

Bringing it over, she sat daintily on the edge of the desk with one arm around my shoulders. 'How did it go with Manzelli?'

'Not quite what I expected. He's quite adamant that he had nothing to do with these slayings — and I believe him. However, he wants me to find the killer before there are any more and also to get him off the hook. You know how touchy he is about not appearing in public and there'd be plenty of exposure if O'Leary did go ahead and have him pulled in for questioning.'

'I can imagine,' she agreed. 'And it wouldn't be too good for you either.'

I sipped the hot coffee trying to put my thoughts into some kind of order. Finally,

I said, 'So who have we got left. I was sure it was Edward Minton but now he's eliminated — in more ways than one.'

There's a link between these victims somewhere but I'm damned if I can see it.

Dawn thought for a while, then asked, 'What do we know about this hoodlum who's now taken over from Cortega? Maybe he was after Cortega's job as head of the outfit. That would be a strong enough motive to kill him and if Barbara Minton happened to witness it he'd have to get rid of her at the same time. It would also explain why your informant was shot in that alley.'

I mulled that over for a couple of minutes; then shook my head. 'But why would he kill that private detective, Baker? That happened before either Cortega and Barbara were murdered.'

She ignored that and went on, 'Perhaps it could also explain why Barbara's husband was also murdered. You said he was well in with Manzelli and possibly Rizzio. If Minton had something on him and was about to spill it to the others — '

I finished my coffee. It burned my throat but enabled me to think more clearly. 'That's pretty far-fetched, Dawn. What was this guy's name — Santos. My guess is he came to L.A. with Cortega just a little while ago. I doubt if Minton knew him. Still, it might be helpful to have a word with him just to clear things up.'

The expression on her face told me she wished she'd never mentioned this guy. 'That would be stupid, Johnny. You managed to get away with it with Cortega. But from what I've heard downtown this gangster is a born killer.'

'These guys are all born killers, Dawn. I've worked with them. I know exactly how they operate.'

'That won't stop you getting a bullet in the back.' She picked up my empty cup and walked back to her desk. 'My advice is to stay well away from him.' She paused and then continued in a low voice, 'Still, you never take my advice about anything. You'll just go your own way and damn the consequences.'

I knew she was right in both respects.

I'd go to see this hoodlum and I'd probably find big trouble.

* * *

Locating Santos wasn't easy but then he didn't intend it should be — especially for nosy private eyes like Johnny Merak. I asked a lot of discreet questions of guys I figured might know of his whereabouts but drew a blank every time. Very soon I was beginning to think that the guy didn't exist. Then, as I was beginning to give up, I struck lucky — but not in the way I expected. I'd just pulled up in a narrow back street in an area of town I'd never been before.

Lighting a cigarette I wound down the window. The inside of the car was almost as hot as the hinges of Hell but even with the window open it was only a little cooler. I'd taken only a couple of drags on the cigarette when the door was suddenly wrenched open. I instinctively reached for the .38 but before I could get it out I found myself staring into a gun barrel lined up with my forehead.

The guy behind it was built like a mountain — definitely not the type you messed around with.

Thrusting his free hand through the window he expertly lifted my gun from its holster and pushed it into his pocket. There was a leering grin on his face that showed a row of broken teeth. I figured he'd never won a beauty contest in his life.

'Move over into the other seat,' he grated. He pushed the gun forward to emphasize his words.

I did as he said and somehow he slid his bulk behind the wheel.

'If this is a heist I've got nothing of value,' I began; then sucked in a sharp intake of air as the weapon was rammed into my ribs.

'Just keep your mouth shut, buster. We're going for a little ride.'

'May I ask where we're going?'

'To see a friend of yours. Mister Santos — and he doesn't like to be kept waiting.' He put the Merc into gear and turned into the middle of the street, one hand on the wheel.

I sat back, staring through the windscreen. I'd spent all morning trying to find this guy, Santos.

Now, it seemed, he'd found me!

My companion put his foot down, racing across a couple of intersections regardless of any other traffic in the way. Still, it wasn't his car so I guess he wasn't particularly bothered whether the paintwork got scratched.

I'd no idea where we were heading. The buildings on either side of the streets became more run down. Evidently, wherever Santos had his headquarters it wasn't in the affluent part of town. After the hair-raising drive had lasted about a quarter of an hour he suddenly swung the car sharply to the left into a narrow alley. At the far end the road widened into a square. There was a garage in one corner. The rest of the place looked completely deserted.

Switching off the ignition, my mountainous friend grunted. 'All right, Merak. Get out.'

I did as he said. He still had the gun in his fist and he looked the type to use it at the slightest opportunity. Towering over me like the Rock of Gibraltar, he waved the weapon towards a two-storey building on the far side of the square. I walked slowly towards it, feeling the gun hard against my back.

There was a door in the wall. Knocking on it loudly, my companion waited. A couple of minutes later a section of the door slid aside. There was a face just visible in the aperture.

'It's me,' said my companion. 'I've got that private dick with me.'

The other guy said something I couldn't catch and a moment later there was the sound of a key being turned in the lock. The door opened on squealing hinges and I was pushed inside. It was dark inside the building and after the brilliant sunlight I could make out nothing. Only gradually did details emerge.

The placed looked like a deserted warehouse that had recently been reno-vated into what could only be called a dump. There were several guys there either leaning against the bare walls or lounging in rickety chairs. All of them looked like Mexicans.

Then one of them got to his feet and said, 'You'll be the private investigator who did some work for Vinnie Cortega before he was unfortunately killed. Perhaps I should introduce myself. I am Emilio Santos. I understand you've been inquiring about me. As you no doubt understand that makes me curious. So now you're going to tell me why.'

'I'm quite willing to answer your questions,' I said. 'Do you mind if I sit down?'

He indicated one of the empty chairs, waited until I'd seated myself, then lowered himself into the chair a couple of feet away, his eyes drilling into me. Unlike most of the other guys present he was well dressed with jet black hair and dark eyes. A neatly trimmed moustache adorned his upper lip. Only his swarthy skin detracted from good looks.

Leaning forward, he rested his elbows on his knees, studying me minutely. 'I should tell you that I do not like people asking questions about me. Are you working for any of the other outfits operating here?'

'Not the outfits,' I replied.

'Then who are you working for — the police, or perhaps the FBI?'

'Neither.'

He sucked in a deep breath. 'You're being evasive. Answer my question. The men you see here are very good at extracting information and making certain it's the truth.'

I knew exactly what he meant. If I didn't tell him what he wanted to hear I'd be taken to some place where there were no nosy neighbours and they'd use a length of rubber hose on me. It wasn't a pleasant prospect.

Swallowing thickly, I said, 'I assume you've heard of Enrico Manzelli.'

His head came up at that. 'Sure I've heard the name. The Godfather of all the outfits in L.A. What has he got to do with me?'

'Quite a lot I reckon. He runs all of the rackets in L.A. and he doesn't like anyone muscling in. Take my word for it, if you try to go against him you're finished.'

His lips twisted. 'Is that a threat?'

'Not from me,' I said hurriedly. I didn't want him to get the impression that I was one of Manzelli's hitmen come to make sure that he fell into line. 'But if I were you, I'd take it very seriously.'

Placing the tips of his fingers together, he said icily, 'I've come up against men like him in Mexico. He doesn't scare me. Does he scare you, amigos?' He turned his head to glance at the men around him. There was an outburst of laughter. All of them shook their heads.

'Before you go off half-cock,' I put in, 'just remember one thing. Cortega set up this outfit without consulting Manzelli or any of the other bosses. Maybe he figured he was invincible but he's dead now.'

Santos' eye narrowed to mere slits and the expression on his swarthy features turned ugly. 'Are you telling me that Manzelli gave the order for him to be shot?'

I shrugged. 'Who knows what orders Manzelli gives?' Someone is behind all of these murders and if it wasn't Manzelli — then who?'

I could see I was getting to him. He didn't like that possibility and for the first time I could see he was seriously believing that Manzelli was a force to be reckoned with. I had one last question for him. 'Have you — or Cortega — ever sent any threatening messages to Manzelli?'

'Why the hell would I do that? I don't even know the guy apart from what I've heard about him.'

I had the gut-feeling he was telling the truth. But with these guys you could never be sure.

'Then I guess there's not much more I can tell you.' I pushed my chair back a couple of inches and said, 'Can I have my gun back and leave? If you need any more information from me you'll find me in the phone book.'

I expected him to say I wasn't going anywhere but surprisingly, he gave a terse nod. To the man standing a couple of feet away, he said sharply, 'Give him his gun back. As he says, we can always find him if we want him.'

The guy gave me my gun and I stood up. This meeting had gone better than I'd expected but I wouldn't feel really safe until I was back in my office. Glancing down at Santos I said calmly, forcing evenness into my voice, 'Could one of your men accompany me back to where I left my car. This is an area of L.A. I don't know at all.'

Santos' lips twitched into what was meant to be a smile. 'You know, Merak,' he said softly, 'I can't make up my mind about you. Either you're a very brave man or completely stupid. You come looking for me knowing quite well I could see to it you never left. If you ever need a real job that pays well, I might consider giving you one with my outfit.'

'Thanks. But I spent many years in the Organization and now I'm going straight I'd like to stay that way.'

'Suit yourself.' He gave a negligent wave of his arm and the bruiser led me towards the door. Somehow, I figured I'd just escaped a premature exit from this earthly life by the skin of my teeth.

6

The Picture Begins To Emerge

By now I was beginning to run out of suspects. Things weren't going the way I wanted them to go at all. Most of those I'd picked out as suspects were now victims, leaving me with virtually nothing to go on. I felt sure that all of these slayings were the work of one person but whoever he was, he was extremely clever. More and more, the evidence seemed to be pointing at Manzelli. Looked at objectively, he was almost certainly the most cold-blooded killer in L.A. yet the cops had never been able to make any charge against him stick.

Then I got something of a break. It wasn't the kind I really wanted. I'd just got into the office when the telephone rang. It was Lieutenant O'Leary. He sounded as though he'd just got out of bed and wished he'd stayed there.

'That you, Merak?' he asked

'Yes, Lieutenant. What is it this time?'

'Something I reckon you ought to know since you still seem to be involved in this Barbara Minton case.' There was a trace of anger in his voice as he rasped the last bit of the sentence. He'd warned me to stay off this case and the fact I was still pursuing it didn't go down well with him.

'Go on.'

'It seems someone has attempted to take out Mrs. Silworth.'

That was the last thing I'd expected. 'Are you sure?'

'Of course I'm sure. She's in the hospital at this very moment. I've got two men there just in case whoever did it means to finish the job.'

'Where did this happen?' My brain wasn't thinking as coherently as it usually did.

'Right here in L.A.'

Those little mice were telling me there was something here that didn't quite make sense. I said, 'She lives in Colorado, doesn't she? What the hell is she doing here?'

'In case you don't know her daughter's

funeral is taking place here this afternoon. She was apparently on her way to attend it. Her son-in-law is also being buried around the same time but not in the same place. It seems Ophelia Silworth refused to allow them to be buried together.'

'I see. And you say someone made an attempt on her life?'

'That's right. Her husband was driving when it happened but there's no doubt it was her that the killer was after.'

'How can you be so sure of that?'

'Because this limousine came alongside their car on the passenger side. My guess is there was plenty of time to get in at least a couple of shots. But just one shot was fired before it sped off. As good luck would have it the shot got her in the arm. Fortunately it was only a flesh wound otherwise we'd have one more victim to add to the murder list.'

'Is she well enough to talk?'

'She's talking her head off at this moment. That's how we got this information.'

'So has she given any reliable description of the one who did this?'

'Plenty. Her husband saw little of it. Seems it happened so fast and he was concentrating on driving.'

'And what has she said?' I had a funny sinking feeling in my stomach as if I already knew what she'd said.

'The usual description. A tall guy dressed in black with his hat pulled down well over his face.'

'That fits nearly all of the hoods in Los Angeles.'

'I'm aware of that. But she claims there was another guy sitting in the back with the would-be killer. A short fat guy whose description fits only one man I know — Enrico Manzelli!'

There it was again. Another victim trying to pin these slayings on the Big Boss of the Organization. Those little mice in my mind were jumping up and down like a troupe of acrobats now and they were telling me that something didn't smell right. Manzelli had no possible motive to kill Ophelia Silworth that I could think of. This didn't make sense at all.

'Do you believe her story, Lieutenant?' I asked.

There was a long pause as if he were wondering why I'd asked that question. At last, he said harshly, 'Why? Don't you believe it?'

'No, I don't. What motive could he have?'

'With Manzelli he doesn't need a motive. Or maybe this was just a warning of some kind. Even from a speeding car these killers very rarely miss their target.'

'Would you have any objections if I were to talk to her?'

'I've already questioned her and as far as I'm concerned it checks out. Besides, when I left her she was demanding that the doctors just patch her up — that come hell or high water she's going to attend her daughter's funeral. I suggest you stay out of this, Merak. I reckon you've poked your nose into this as far as it'll go before someone chops it off. This is an attempted murder. I'm telling you to leave it to us.' The tone of his voice told me he meant what he said.

He put the phone down leaving me staring at the receiver in my hand. I'd just replaced it when Dawn came in. 'Anything happening, Johnny?' she asked, taking off her coat.

'You might call it that. Someone has apparently tried to finish off Ophelia Silworth.'

She looked shocked. 'How is she?'

'It was just a flesh wound in the arm. Her husband was driving her to the hotel. Her daughter's funeral takes place this afternoon.'

'Do the police know who was responsible?'

'She claims that this car came alongside theirs and just one shot was fired. She also insists that some guy who would only be Manzelli from her description was sitting in the back seat with the gunman.'

She stared at me and then said the same thing as O'Leary. 'But you don't believe her?'

'I think she's lying through her teeth. Why, I don't know.'

She placed a cup of hot coffee on the desk in front of me. 'So how are you going to find out?'

'By asking the right questions of someone who knows what really happened.' I grinned at her scared expression. 'No need to worry. I'm not thinking about Man-zelli. I'm talking about Ophelia's husband.'

'Do you know where he's likely to be?'

'My guess is he's at the hospital with his wife. If I'm right then somehow I have to get him away from her for a few minutes. I need to talk to him alone.'

Dawn looked puzzled but only said, 'Then I'll come with you.'

She expected me to argue but instead, I said, 'I want you to come. You may be able to get into conversation with Ophelia if she insists on joining her husband.'

Less than twenty minutes later we arrived at the hospital. I expected some trouble with the Silworths but the first hitch I encountered was with the receptionist, a frosty-faced dame in her fifties who insisted that Mr. and Mrs. Silworth were to see no one without the doctor's permission. At the moment he was attending to his patient who had a nasty bullet wound in her arm and had lost quite a lot of blood.

'Then is it possible to speak with Mr. Silworth alone — just for a few minutes?' I asked politely.

'Are you relatives of theirs?' she demanded, evidently determined to do everything according to the rules.

Keeping my temper, I said, 'Look, this is a case of attempted murder' I took out my business card and pushed it across the desk. 'I'm investigating it on behalf of Lieutenant O'Leary of the Homicide Squad.' That wasn't strictly true and I knew I'd probably be in deep trouble if she decided to phone O'Leary.

She glanced at my card and then handed it back. She seemed no longer quite so sure of herself.

Finally, she said, 'Very well. If you go along that corridor, it's the last door on the left.'

Taking Dawn by the arm I hustled her along the corridor. 'Let's see if we can find Silworth before that receptionist decided to check with O'Leary,' I said.

The door was half open when we reached it. Ophelia Silworth was there with her back to us talking to a guy in a white coat. They seemed to be having some kind of argument but they kept their voices down so I couldn't make out any of the words.

Then Dawn touched my arm and pointed. A short distance away was an open space with chairs along the sides. In one of them sat an elderly man with greying hair. Going forward, I asked softly,

'Excuse me but are you Mr. Silworth?'

He looked up quickly, then nodded. 'That's my name,' he replied. 'May I ask who you are?'

'I'm a private investigator,' I told him. 'My name's Merak. I'm investigating the circumstances surrounding your daughter's murder. May I have a few words with you?'

A strange expression flashed across his face — fear, suspicion, surprise — it was impossible to tell.

'I don't understand what you want with me. I thought they'd arrested her husband for the killing.'

'Since he, too, was shot and my guess is by the same man, I don't think the police believe that.'

'Then what is it you want from me?'

'I'd like you to tell me exactly what happened this morning when your wife was with you in your car. The police have told me that a black limousine came up alongside you and someone fired one shot at your wife? Is that what happened?'

He ran his tongue around his lips as if his mouth had suddenly gone dry. Clearing his throat he said harshly, 'I saw very little of what happened. There was a lot of traffic around and I had to concentrate on driving. I didn't even hear the sound of the shot.'

'No you wouldn't. It's certain that whoever did this used a silencer. Your wife also gave what was an extremely accurate description of a passenger in that car. Now if I saw a gun pointed at me from a couple of feet away my first instinct would be to duck but your wife sat there apparently quite calmly and was able to take in every detail of the other guy who was even further away from her than this assassin. Not only that but this second man would be almost completely hidden by the first.'

His lips twisted in sudden anger, Silworth said savagely, 'Are you suggesting that my wife is deliberately lying to the police, Merak?'

'That's what I'm trying to find out.'

Silworth got to his feet and for a moment I thought he meant to hit me. Somehow, he managed to control himself. 'I think you'd better go before I have the security throw you out — and if you repeat any of this to anyone I'll see that you lose your licence and never work as an investigator again.'

'You're bluffing, Silworth. For one thing you're not a resident of California so I doubt if you'll have any say as to whether I lose my licence or not. My guess is you're hiding something and no matter what you do or say I sure as hell will find out what it is.'

The expression on his face told me that my shot had gone home. If he could've turned any whiter he'd have shone like the driven snow. I turned and walked quickly back along the corridor, leaving him staring after me, possibly wondering just how much I knew.

Beside me, Dawn said in a low voice, 'What do you think, Johnny?'

'I'm not sure. He could be telling the truth. His story tallies almost exactly with that of his wife. But there's something he doesn't want me to know.'

Dawn thought for a moment; then said, 'Do you think we might learn more if we were to attend the funeral this afternoon?'

'I reckon that's a good idea. I'd like you to come with me again. You might spot something I miss.' She looked pleased at that.

*　*　*

There was a whole fleet of limousines at the cemetery when we got there. It looked as if half of the state of Colorado had turned up to say a final farewell to Barbara. I guessed that several of the folk there had come from L.A. as well. Evidently Mrs. Silworth intended that her daughter would have as big a send off as possible.

I parked the Merc some distance from the assembled crowd. Dawn and I got out and stood in the shadow of a tall elm where we had a clear view of everyone. As I'd guessed, Lieutenant O'Leary was present together with Sergeant Kolowinski. They stood well away from the others.

They were some distance from where we stood but I knew O'Leary had spotted us and he was probably there for the same reason as ourselves.

There was an old saying that a murderer always visits the funeral of his victim. From past experience I'd come to rely on it but picking out the murderer among the gathering was far from simple. The one I was after was clever, very clever.

Ophelia stood close to the head of the grave. Her right arm was bandaged and in a sling. Her husband stood beside her his face impassive. He was staring down at his feet and never lifted his head once during the whole proceedings. Just behind them stood someone else I recognized — Lieutenant Morgan. I couldn't figure out what he was doing there until I recalled that he'd been a close friend of Edward Minton.

Since he was also due to be buried here I figured Morgan would be attending both funerals. We waited until the coffin had been lowered into the ground and the mourners were drifting away towards the

cars before moving over towards the far
side of the cemetery. The second fleet of
limousines accompanying Edward Minton's body was just moving in from the
other gate. There weren't as many here as
had been at Barbara's graveside but then
I figured that Ophelia Silworth wasn't
interested in her son-in-law — at least not
now he was dead.

'Did you notice anyone back there who
looked at all suspicious?' I asked, turning
to Dawn.

She shook her head. 'No one unless it
was that man standing immediately
behind Ophelia.'

'That was Lieutenant Morgan, a close
friend of not only Edward Minton but
also Manzelli.'

She looked shocked but said nothing
more. There were only a few cars on the
wide path near where Minton was to be
buried. There were, however, a couple of
the usual black limousines from the
Organization and seven guys got out and
moved close to where the minister stood
at the head of the grave.

'It would seem that Manzelli has sent a

few of his boys to pay his last respects,' I said to Dawn, keeping my voice down. 'Apart from Morgan I don't recognize any of the others. I'm beginning to think we're wasting our time here.'

Dawn surveyed the small crowd and then asked, 'Who's that man over there?'

She inclined her head toward a little guy standing near one of the trees on the edge of the cemetery. I studied him closely. I recognized him at once from the old days. Tiny Matson, a hit man for the Mob. A snappy dresser with a soft hat pulled well down over his eyes, He had a thin, angular face with close-set eyes that took in everything.

'Don't let him see you watching him, Dawn,' I whispered hastily.

'Why? Do you know him?'

'I know him well enough. He's a professional killer. As far as I'm aware he doesn't belong to any of the regular outfits. They just call on him whenever they want a job doing. If the price is right he'll do the job for anyone.'

Dawn sucked in a deep breath. 'Then what is he doing here?'

'That,' I said harshly, 'is what I'd like to know. There's some reason for it but I'm damned if I know what it is. I doubt if he'll try anything here. Not with the law present over yonder.' I inclined my head towards O'Leary and the Sergeant who'd now moved to a spot about a hundred yards away from us.

We waited until the minister had completed the service. All the time I kept my eye on the little fellow. He hadn't moved an inch. Then he suddenly turned quickly on his heel and strode off in the direction of the main gate.

Grabbing Dawn's arm I whispered. 'Let's go. I want to follow him and see where he goes. First, I need a word with O'Leary.' I hurried over to where he was standing.

'You here to express your condolences, Merak? Or is there some other reason for your presence?' he asked thinly.

'There's no time to explain, Lieutenant.' I said hurriedly. 'Tiny Matson is here and I reckon I can now lead you to the person behind these murders. But I need you to follow me and be on the scene when I do.'

For once he was quick on the uptake and didn't argue. 'All right, Merak. But this had better be good.'

I could see that he was puzzled but he said nothing more as he and Kolowinski fell into step with us. Reaching the Merc I slid behind the wheel as Dawn crushed in beside me. The two cops got into the back. Our quarry went over to a car parked just outside the gates and got in.

Switching on the ignition I eased the Merc forward slowly, giving him time to get some distance ahead of us. I didn't think he'd recognized me back there. I'd only had contact with him on a couple of occasions and that had been a long time ago but I didn't intend to take any chances. These guys were professionals. But so was I and I had the feeling that if he led us to where I figured he would be headed a lot of the scattered little pieces of the puzzle might fall neatly into place.

There wasn't too much traffic about at that time and it was easy to keep him in sight as he led us into the residential part of town. Very soon I knew my hunch had paid off. I'd been this way once before when Edward Minton had been shot. As I expected, Tiny's car turned into the drive, stopping at the end. I noticed the front door open as he got out.

'Evidently he's expected,' I said. I waited until the door closed before putting my foot down on the accelerator and speeding towards the house. We skidded to a halt. To O'Leary I said sharply, 'I reckon we'd better be careful, Lieutenant. Tiny is the type to use his gun and ask questions later and he's not too keen on the law. It might be wise if the Sergeant were to go around the back just in case Tiny should decide to flee the joint.'

I walked up to the door and rang the bell. I'd already guessed who was inside. The door opened and Mrs. Silworth stood there. There was a blend of surprise and shock on her face as she saw me.

Then she somehow pulled herself together. 'May I ask what you're doing here, Mister Merak?'

The acid in her voice would have melted a hole through a steel pipe.

Without giving her a chance to say anything further I pushed her aside, motioning the others to follow me. I heard her utter a high-pitched yell as I pulled the .38 from its holster just as Tiny Matson burst into sight at the end of the passage. He had a gun in his hand and I didn't hesitate. I pulled the trigger and the gun dropped from his fingers as the slug smashed his wrist. A moment later the rear door was kicked open and Kolowinski thrust his way inside.

O'Leary pushed Ophelia into the hallway. A minute later we were all inside the large front room.

Tiny was dripping blood onto the floor as Kolowinski cuffed him. His face was an ugly grey and he was moaning deep in his throat.

'I think I should tell you that I intend to make a formal complaint to your superiors, Lieutenant. You have no right forcing your way in here without a warrant. I've just buried my daughter and I — '

She dabbed melodramatically at her eyes with her handkerchief.

'I'm afraid those crocodile tears don't

wash with me,' I said sharply.

'Just what are you getting at, Merak?' O'Leary snapped.

Staring straight at Ophelia, I said, 'I reckon I've got most of this whole affair figured out but correct me if I'm wrong. You shot James Baker, the private investigator your son-in-law hired to dig up the dirt on your daughter. As for the rest of these murders, my guess is that you hired our friend with the smashed wrist to carry them out. You knew he was a professional killer willing to do any job at a price and keep his mouth shut.'

I thought she was going to utter a vehement denial but instead she clamped her lips even tighter.

Going on, I said, 'That's why he's here to collect payment.' To the Lieutenant, I added, 'I think you'll find a cheque for quite a large sum in his pocket, made out by her.'

O'Leary went over and thrust his hand into Tiny's inside pocket, pulling out a slip of paper. He nodded, 'Three hundred thousand dollars,' he said crisply. 'I reckon that clinches it. But what made you think of her as Baker's killer and why kill all the others?'

'Somehow she discovered that her son-in-law had hired him to follow Barbara and she couldn't allow this scandal to come out into the open. Baker was finding out too much and had to be disposed of. But she made one mistake. That same day she phoned me asking if there was any truth in the rumour that Baker had been murdered.'

Glancing across at her, I asked, 'How could you possibly know it was murder? Our first conclusion was that he'd committed suicide. The landlord couldn't have known because he'd gone by the time I'd discovered he couldn't possibly have shot himself. The Lieutenant here might have told you, but I told you to phone him after you'd spoken to me. As I see it, the only way you could have known would be if you shot him yourself and then carried out the switch with his gun and yours.'

The expression on her face told me I'd got it right first time.

'And the other killings?' O'Leary queried.

'Basically, I think she held a deep hatred for the Organization. She knew her son-in-law was in with them. She also knew her daughter was mixed in with the Mobs when she got in with Cortega. I'm also quite sure that Barbara stole a fortune in diamonds which she hid in that petrol can we found in the wreckage, intending to give them to her boy friend. After having both Barbara and Ortega killed she finally went the whole way and had Minton shot. I think all of these were committed by Tiny here on her orders. I also think she was responsible for sending threatening letters to a certain friend of mine. I intend to let him know that. Somehow I figure she'll be safer on death row than on the streets once he knows that.'

I looked at Silworth, sitting there with his hands clasped in his lap. He seemed like a lost soul in Purgatory desperately looking for a way out. 'All three of them were working together,' I said, 'although I doubt if Mister Silworth had any heart for it. I think if the D.A. was to accept a shorter sentence for him instead of the chair, he'll spill everything, Lieutenant.'

'And that attack where she was wounded in the arm?' Dawn spoke for the first time.

'All planned. These hitmen very seldom miss their target, especially from such close range. My guess is her husband did it just to throw off any possible suspicion.'

'All right, Merak. You've convinced me.' O'Leary motioned to the three to get up. 'I guess this case is closed.'

'There's one thing you can do for me, Lieutenant.'

'Oh, what's that?'

'There's a hoodlum called Santos running a protection racket on the east side. I figure the city would be a lot better off if he was either pulled in or run out of town.'

O'Leary thought hard and then nodded. 'I'll see what I can do. If he was implicated in the killing of that guy in the alley beside Mancini's it shouldn't be too difficult.'

★　★　★

Back in the office I put through a call on Manzelli's number. As I'd guessed it was one of his boys who answered. Briefly, I explained all that had happened and that the person who'd been sending him the anonymous threatening letters was no longer a threat to him. The guy listened but never said a word. The line went dead but I knew the message would reach Manzelli as sure as the Mississippi ended up in the ocean.

It was two days later when Dawn came in with the post. There was only one letter with my name on the envelope. Opening it I took out the single slip of paper. Whistling thinly through my teeth, I handed it to Dawn.

It was a cheque for twenty-five thousand dollars and it was one cheque I knew for sure wouldn't bounce.

It had Enrico Manzelli's name written in black ink at the bottom!

THE END

SEND FOR DR. MORELLE

Ernest Dudley

Mrs. Lorrimer telephones Doctor Morelle claiming that she's in imminent mortal danger. In the morning her orange drink was poisoned, then she'd found a deadly snake in her bed and now toxic gas is emanating from the chimney and into the room! But is she really in danger? Is she mad — or perhaps feigning madness? Dutifully, Doctor Morelle sets off to the woman's house with Miss Frayle, his long-suffering assistant, who will soon begin to wish she'd stayed behind . . .

DR. MORELLE ELUCIDATES

Ernest Dudley

Dr. Morelle expounds on seven puzzling cases in his inimitable manner. For *The Case of the Man Who Was Too Clever*, the doctor and his assistant Miss Frayle investigate the murder of an actress, whose dying screams are the clue to her death. Whilst in *The Case of the Clever Dog*, a murder is committed in the doctor's presence, but man's best friend is the clue in finding the killer . . .

THE G-BOMB

John Russell Fearn

The cleverest man
Glebe, becomes the
baleful intelligence.
G-Bomb, should
himself and his dau
instead it brings de
threat to mankind
knows the danger, b
— framed for Marg
release comes too l
cataclysm engulfing
fate decrees that h
little man from drov
changes destiny . . .